Flight Advice
a fabulary

stories by Tobey Hiller

Unlikely Books
www.UnlikelyStories.org
New Orleans, Louisiana

Flight Advice: a fabulary

Fifteen Dollars US

ISBN: 979-8-9851371-2-5

Library of Congress Control Number: 2021949696

Unlikely Books
www.UnlikelyStories.org
New Orleans, Louisiana

Flight Advice
a fabulary

I no longer know whether the events I am about to relate are effects or causes.

—Jorge Luis Borges

The Order in Which They Appear

Down by the Riverside

Story has lost his way. He knocks on a door, and someone lets him in. Inside, there is a hall with many mirrors that make it seem he is walking into his own reflection walking into his reflection, walking into...

He stops to think. Years ago there would have been many doors in here; behind one, a lush garden from whose leaves issued an irresistible sound of woodwinds, behind another a woman in a skirt made of brambles spinning a thread of gold, behind another the pitch and roll of the sea with almost at the horizon a pirate ship, or over there a veil or patch of fog behind which the moans and motion of love, or torture, could just barely be made out... Or at least a gaggle of ragged children plucking rice out of the cavities in a porous rock—something to work with.

He looks closely at a shadow in the corner of a mirror to his left, and the shadow blots itself into a looming figure in a dark suit, holding up a small toothed gadget, who says, "This handy little all-in-one tool will slice a cucumber, julienne a carrot, dice a zucchini, or even (snicker) ball a melon..."

Abruptly, Story pulls away. For this, he thinks, I sharpened my pen to a sword-sharp point and learned how to speak 181 languages? Or was that 1,081? Hard to remember, since the words will follow any Open Sesame into the nearest jar and leak out the bottom like water. He goes out a back door squashed almost to a beanstalk width between two mirrors, a splinter of an exit just large enough to squeeze through. The narrowness of the niche scrapes his skin, reminding him of the pains of transformation.

He can remember a time when he was her and rode clothed in her own hair. Camels were her favorite conveyance. She lived in a tree, or under a pillow on a glass mountain, or in a hut constructed of cannonballs and straw, an unstable combination, but it did keep the wind out.

She comes out into the back yard and stands under a tree, looking through leaves at the sky. Where are the gods? Where in fact are the birds?

Cars whiz by somewhere nearby.

She hears buzzing and wonders: is that an apiary, a distant chainsaw, or the crackle of a chain reaction?

Story wishes she still had her coat of many colors and then remembers she does still have a pennywhistle. She takes it out and begins to play, the melody full of plaint and foreboding, but no one comes.

They are all somewhere else, she guesses, with their thumbs tied to pixels and their ear-buds in. This reminds her that she's forgotten how to spell, and so, putting her whistle back in her pocket, where it nestles down next to her skipping stone, she takes off to look for a dictionary. Or a Border Collie.

However, she becomes distracted by a sign advertising 31 flavors of ice cream, though the sign is more like a movie screen than a poster. This makes her think of that circus story she used to know—what was it called? Cinderella? The Three Stooges? Something about the Dutch Mountains?—and anyway, 31 doesn't sound like the right number—she was sure it was supposed to be seven, or 1001, wasn't it? In any case, it's always flesh, not ice cream. She says this out loud, rather loudly. Whereupon some men in uniforms swoop down upon her. She is arrested for vagrancy and possible lewd behavior and put in the county jail.

Here there is plenty of light, all electric of course, but no books and only microwaved food, along with no backtalk. Since her conversation is mainly backtalk, before very long she is put in solitary confinement. But she still has a few tricks up her sleeve, so she skips her stone and hightales it out of there, ending up down by the riverside, with the homeless kids and the drunks.

She likes it here and decides to spend the night. It's familiar because of the open fires, telling their endless tales of flicker and pull, the nomad saunter from one motion to another, compelling spots of bright among the improvisations of tents and cardboard shelters. Sudden glow and portability – it's a longterm thing. Also she likes the glittering eyes she sees here and there, so like stars. Not to mention the encroaching darkness. Possibilities, with their dark and hungry mouths. In the morning she wakes up with tattoos on both her forearms and a memory of all of Thunder Semen and Roving Spirochete's songs. She remembers being in the belly of a whale. Or was that a ship? She remembers chains. Also she has some cuts and a flowering bruise or two, but this is nothing new.

She leaves the camp the next morning, wearing the shortest words she can find around her throat and in her ears. Tomorrow, she thinks, I'll learn three dying languages, some whale song and tree pantoum, and try that thing that Proteus did. I think I used to love it.

The Seventh Blue

One

On the outskirts of town, a young man who's not where he should be encounters a mangy-looking black dog nosing around in the municipal garbage dump. The dog comes up, looking friendly, and the young man, stretching his hand out idly to be sniffed, notices something blue on its neck. Looking closer, he discovers a large blue stone peeking out from the greasy black hair at the base of the dog's cranium. It's seemingly set in the bone of the skull itself. The thing glitters; sun bounces off it into his eyes, splintering his thought into something like tinder or debris. Unconsciously he has taken a step back, fingers tingling. Is it a disease? Could it actually be a gem?

In the explosive noon light, he wonders briefly whether the dog is a ghost or dream, but when the animal, smelling hotly of doghair and afternoon, continues standing there, its tongue lolling out between its teeth, panting, his thought takes a different turn. How priceless the skull of a dog with an embedded precious stone must undoubtedly be. How scientists, collectors—people like that—people looking for proofs or miracles, would scramble after the unlikeliness of it, their wallets disgorging green... and then as he stands there it seems to him his luck, frequently unreliable, has suddenly improved. His mind closes tight around the stone, or better, the skull with the stone still stuck in it. He begins talking to the dog in a wheedling tone, intending to lure it toward his truck. He has a rifle stowed under the seat. But the dog hangs back, peers at him suspiciously. Suddenly it shies off and lopes away toward town.

Sweat pops out on the young man's palms and forehead. He hightails it back to his truck and drives fast into town, where he just manages to catch a glimpse of the dog disappearing into the leafy shadow of a main avenue. He runs a stop sign and makes a blind pass around a truck to keep up. Loping steadily, the dog turns two corners and crosses a large square, leaving his pursuer, cursing and leaning helplessly on his horn, mired in traffic on the far side. Now the dog, who has begun to look to the young man more and more like one of those dawns you've already and irrevocably slept through, turns into a side street called Lilac. By the time his pursuer, now beet red and panting, turns down this street, the dog has trotted up the front path of a certain house and round to the shady garden in back, where the lady of the house, a solitary woman well past youth, is sitting on her back porch, shelling peas. Her name, as it happens, is Anna.

Hearing an animal panting, she looks up from the bowl in her lap just as a truck drives by in front, fast. "Here, boy," she says without even thinking, forgetting the noisy and multiple discouragements of middle age, and holds out her hand. The black dog drops his head and wags his tail, and five minutes later he's inside her kitchen eating a bowl of scraps. She calls him Nero, for the obvious reason, and although she immediately notices the blue stone, it doesn't surprise her or put her off particularly. She thinks of it as a carbuncle, a tumor, nothing else, and feels sorry for him that his noble head is thus marked, so that he must carry a sign of life's dangers and injustices on his scalp, making him a creature not quite innocent, but also, by virtue of this very injury to his nature, completely himself.

Nero, as she calls him, though before this a vagabond, settles down happily with her, and the upshot is that he lives out the rest of his life quite happily in her house -- a matter of eating scraps every day in her kitchen, dozing by her warm hearth in the winter, and panting, eyes half-closed, in her back yard on hot summer days. All this time he carries the blue carbuncle, which neither grows nor shrinks, on his head. Anna treats him as friend and companion. She tells him her dreams in the morning and counts the day's events to him at night. To her, his life is unblemished and comforting, and for his part he never strays. When he finally dies, she digs him a grave under a tree in the back yard and puts a smooth white rock there, to remember him.

She herself dies some years later at an advanced age, leaving the house to a favorite niece, who moves in at once, overjoyed to leave her mother's dominion and grateful for the soft greenness of her aunt's lawn, for the pear tree, for the cool upstairs bedrooms where a breeze blows on even the hottest nights. Being young and eager, she changes all the furniture around at once and paints everything a different color. In due time, she marries. She and her husband—for they are both hard workers and do everything with thoroughness and a hurrying hope—soon have three children and a house full of noise and laundry and enterprise in all its stages.

One day their youngest child, a dreamy boy named Nicanor, who is often left to himself because his older brothers consider him too young to be interesting and not quite pliable enough to be useful, is rolling a ball around in the back yard. His eye catches a gleam of odd blue in the irises. (Now the iris bed is a good way from the white stone, which still lies, after all these years, under the pear tree, but the earth can carry things along underground in its veins just as a river carries rocks. No doubt you are familiar with how things without wings or feet sometimes travel). Nicanor investigates, finds a smooth piece of something sky-colored sticking up out of the soil, and digs up the blue stone where it lies among the bulbous roots of the iris. If there are any dog bones or skulls about, Nicanor doesn't notice them. The stone he has found is between the size of a chicken's egg and a tennis ball. Perhaps it has grown in the ground, since it was only the size of a frog's eye or a golf ball, at most, when the black dog carried it from the garbage dump to Anna's house.

Nicanor doesn't show this treasure to his two brothers, because he's learned that anything of value will migrate from his hand to theirs if he's not careful. Nor does he take it to his mother, because he doesn't want to be told its name—he's already named it in his mind—or what to do with it. Nor to his father, because his father doesn't have time and stares off into the evening sky with many plans written on his forehead, right above his frown. The name Nicanor has given the stone is his own secret name, the one known only to him. He puts the stone in a secret place, where no one else will find it. In two years, he has forgotten both the name of the stone and where he has hidden it.

The stone's hiding place is behind a loose board in a certain corner of his room. It lies enclosed and unseen for seven years, while Nicanor forgets everything he knew up to the day he found the stone, and finds out other things. When he is thirteen he jumps up to touch the ceiling in his bedroom, wrapped in the tall soft thought of touching his girlfriend's breast, and bumps the wall just so. The rock falls out of the wall, kerplunk. It bounces off his bed and comes to rest on the floor at his feet.

He thinks it is a piece of the planet plastic, or possibly, the moon. He thinks it is a piece of a cat's eye, something his auntie always told him could fall out of a certain midnight on to your head and change the course of your life. He thinks it is a sign that he will be his country's best soccer player and discover an island as yet uncharted in the southern seas.

He decides, after picking it up and examining it closely, that it is too beautiful to keep and so, the next night—that is, as soon as he can—he gives the stone to his girlfriend, to whom all beautiful things, in his estimation, are due, as are rewards to virtue, wine to wildness, rivers to the sea. Not once since it rolled out of his wall has he remembered that the name he gave it before was his own.

The stone frightens his girlfriend, whose name is Ariane. It does not look like turquoise, or sapphire, or actually anything at all she has seen before. It sits on her night table and glows in the dark. Or at least, whether or not it glows, she finds it hard, when the lights are out, not to look at the place it must occupy in space. She believes she hears it talking to her after midnight. She is afraid it has a secret name, or possibly a whole list of them. Every night, when it looks at her, she can't sleep.

Three days later, she goes to the seashore with Nicanor's best friend. She takes the blue stone along. It is evening, and there are many stars, some of them floating on the dark breast of the sea. Below them the surf grumbles and nibbles at the stones buttressing the headlands. They lie down at the grassy edge of the cliff. When they kiss, neither one of them knows who planned it or remembers daytime, exactly. Ariane feels the blue stone, cold and reminding, against her leg. She turns quickly, squirming out of the embrace, and throws the thing into the sea. She doesn't know whether she is more angry at Nicanor for giving her this blue stone which neither one of them can name and both would like to give away, or angry at herself for throwing his gift, glowing and too heavy, into the sea. After this she is not Nicanor's girlfriend anymore.

Alternate #1 (*Two*)

Nicanor, of course, grows up. (Time's flow, though perhaps flexible in quantum physics, is irrevocably downstream here; this current carries Nicanor, as well as you and me, into the midst of it). He does not quite forget Ariane, who threw away his heart, but the yearning in the memory no longer exactly belongs to her. It has become a smoke inhabiting a certain patch of headlands, a leap upward into space, a tearing out of something that falls, heavy as a piece of midnight moon, on the foot that would have taken him to soccer glory, or to Mars. What he does forget, and completely, is the blue stone. He does not become a soccer player, or an explorer; he becomes a teacher in a school for children with special problems, and he derives much real pleasure from his work, which he does well. He marries and has two children of his own, a boy and a girl, and along the way he teaches himself accounting and tax preparation in order to enhance his income, because money is always tight, and life expensive.

One day he stops at the market on the way home to buy a fish for supper. At home, he's reading the newspaper, his wife is cooking dinner and the kids are playing cave under the dining table, when his wife comes out of the kitchen carrying a blue stone the size of a goose egg. "Look at this," she says. "Look what I found in the fish you bought."

Their little girl runs up. "Oh, oh, oh," she says, "how beautiful, how beautiful! Whose is it?"

"Well, now it's ours, because the sea sent it here," says his wife, holding her hand out, her palm cupped beautifully around the stone, so the child can see. Nicanor, though he does not know why, finds this answer peculiarly satisfying, and sees quite clearly as she says it not only why he loves her but a small blue house situated by the sea with irises growing on the roof and a walkway of white stones, a place not quite like any place he ever lived but one he remembers, with utter certainty, as his own.

Alternate #1 different (*Three*)

One day years later a fisherman who is Nicanor's poker buddy sees a disturbing sight at the sea shore. He could swear, he tells his poker mates, it was a dolphin with a crown. Or maybe, christ almighty, it was a mermaid, the way they always used to say you'd see them, on certain clear days when the sea was greenish. Not to say he believes in mermaids. Likely it was dolphins they saw when they said mermaids. Anyway, it was something, not some mirage or figment, he would swear on anything you pleased it was actually there, and he hadn't been drinking either. The crown had a big blue stone, and the dolphin, damn it, dancing and cavorting just like a refugee from some fairy tale—which by the way was not his favorite kind of literature—got up on its tail in the waves near the shore, and, with a leap no earthly dolphin had ever made in his sight before, threw the crown, or whatever it was, at the beach. When he ran over he found a ring of shells and a blue stone in the sand. At this point in the story he puts a real blue stone in the middle of the table, along with the chips and the coins that lie there, and Nicanor experiences a faint shock of recognition. It seems familiar, that stone, though he can't think where he has seen it before.

The stone lies there, and no one picks it up.

"I wonder what that's called," says someone, meaning, turquoise or lapis or agate or what.

"Stachis," says Nicanor, and knows at the same time that he has forgotten something important. The stone follows him home by means of his friend, who leaves it on his doorstep wrapped in a note which says that since he knows the name of the thing, he should have it.

Four

So the blue stone has been thrown into the sea by a boy's sweetheart. Let's leave mermaids and dolphins on their tails out of it. It's a stone that travels best embedded in bone.

One day a black dog comes trotting out of the foam. (Only you see it. There's no one at all on the beach.) The dog's fur is wet, and it's panting as though it has swum a long way or been underwater. Between its ears and embedded in its skull is a blue stone about as big as a goose egg. Perhaps it has other names than the secret one, belonging to himself, which Nicanor gave it and then forgot, but if so, they are invisible and unheard, for they are written nowhere upon it. It comes out of the water a stone in a dog's head.

What is it that determines whether Nicanor will ever see it again? You might say the story. You might say the author. You might say the habits and longings of the reader. You might say chance, or order, various structural factors that rule the possibilities.

Whatever you say, the black dog is there now, where you are and where I am, trotting along the beach (it is a generic beach) with wet fur. His fur smells in that doggy way. He has already shaken himself, water spraying outward in shivers of splatter that look, briefly, like iridescent quills in the sun and leave, when they fall, little pocks of wetness on the sand.

The story simply trots along, going somewhere as yet invisible, carrying this blue stone in its head. A travelling stone which so far has shed any name given it.

Nicanor is not on the beach. He is in his study, dreamily staring out the window. He is not thinking of beaches or dogs or stones. If you could see his thought, it might look familiar to you, in color, say, or motion. He is thinking, if he is thinking of anything, of his loneliness, which is a loneliness not made of solitude, for he has a family and a job and all the attendant connections and pre-occupations. This feeling, a yearning, is one in which he feels curiously at home, though it bears no resemblance to happiness and is kin to—but not quite the same as—sorrow.

The story has dissolved into the no-thingness of thought. Only the stone in the head of the dog is blue, blue as the sea on the kind of seaside day you desire, blue as the hands of dead men, blue as the thought of blue you carry behind your forehead.

(5)

Blue.

Violent Story (*Six*)

A man with a knife is seen walking along the beach toward the dog. He is perhaps the same man, older now, who first tried to wheedle the black dog toward his car when he saw him walk out of the trash heap. Or perhaps his brother. In any case he has intentions and a story of his own.

But when he sees the dog trotting toward him on the sand he sees the stone at once, though for just the first instant he thinks he is seeing a menacing black dog with a hole in its head through which a bit of blue sea shows. Synonymous with the realization that it is a blue stone comes the intention to possess the stone and the idea that he will kill the dog to get it.

He drops the flame of his intention low to keep the signal of it from spooking the animal and walks more casually and slowly down the beach but still toward the dog, his face turned toward the sea. As the dog trots closer, it drops its head and stops, as though sniffing at an invisible set of tracks. The man is now within ten feet of the dog. Suddenly he darts forward, his knife up; at precisely the same moment the dog rises from the sand like a black comet, snarling, and fastens its teeth in his throat. The man stabs and stabs again. He staggers. There's blood in the air and in his eyes, and he cannot hear the sea. A terrible shaking occurs, and then he is aware of sand in his eyes. A complete silence enters him.

The dog has killed him. He lies in the sand, his mouth and eyes and throat open, the sky dead to him. There is no one to see this, but you. The dog is bleeding, too, from wounds in its side. The surf pounds. The knife lies in the sand. The dog resumes its trot down the beach, bleeding, but it is not going to die today.

Is it the stone which killed the man, or the dog? Or was it his intention, and the fear that made him see a dog with a hole in its head through which the sea was eyeing him?

In this version the comforting lady does not appear and we have forgotten Nicanor. Our specie shape is bleeding through the hole in the dog's head, which is a stone.

Seven

The dog turns east and leaves the beach, passing down a long deserted road running through willows and scrub toward a small town. As he passes a scattering of farms, another dog - a shepherd - comes out of a field and follows him. At the next farm, a mutt part Labrador, comes out into the road, barks twice, and joins the other two. Goats and cows and sheep and other barnyard animals, fowl and pigs, stop chewing or scratching, and stand looking. Cats observe, carefully motionless except for their tails. By the time the black dog with blood on its coat and the blue stone in its skull hits the outskirts of town, there are eight dogs following him. Soon there are more.

Dogs come out of backyards, down side streets. They whine and whine, scratching at the back door, till someone lets them out to run through the yard and join what is at first a pack but quickly becomes a horde. The street is now full of dogs trotting and panting, all going in the same direction, and people have noticed. They turn and stare. Owners of dogs take action. They whistle and call: "Here, Toby! Here Buster!" but the sound of these whistles and cries no longer seems to make ordinary sense and the dogs do not respond. Animal control officers, the police and eventually even the fire department are called, and men in uniform mill around looking official and issuing orders, but these measures have no effect. After a while there's a growing commotion, a confused shouting and brandishing of weapons and implements, with occasional snarls and barks from the dogs. But these are the town dogs, familiar, everyone's pets and neighbors' pets; no one wants to shoot or snare them—at the same time, there are too many, and it is too strange, for people to feel comfortable wading into the throng. The dogs themselves do not look from side to side or run here and there sniffing, as dogs in packs often do. They trot forward as though yesterday has disappeared from their territory.

Now the dogs have begun to look strange to the people watching, as though they have lost the terms of recognition, as though their own dogs have become a cloud of locusts or a nomadic tribe with strange head dresses. Occasionally there are still plaintive or irritable calls from dog owners, of names no longer effective, but mostly people have gotten quiet and begun to stay clear of the margins of this exodus, recognizing, though without understanding it, the truth. The dogs trot out of town, following the dog with the stone in his skull. Perhaps he is the dog king. Perhaps he has a paradisical smell. Perhaps they have heard a sound invisible to human beings.

All of these dogs disappear for good. The owners do not hear of them again. Nobody knows where they have gone. Some people think it's a plot.

They turn up next in Ariane's dream. Ariane has grown up to be a singer of some renown. She lives in a desert place and has a fine, deep contralto voice with tragic over-tones. She sings songs of discarded and difficult love, of midnight and empty streets, of dancing alone under moons thinking of you. The place she lives and the quality of her voice have opposing effects on the number of her visitors—while one effectively keeps many away, the other ensures that a few, particularly lovesick young men, will persevere in their attempts to reach her home and test her reputation, which is mottled. This opposition would probably lack any tension if she were not also beautiful, with long dark hair and a sultry and challenging air. Some of the young men come and merely wait, standing outside her house, under a tree or by the well, hoping that she'll come out to draw water, or sing. But Ariane herself drinks principally wine, and only her cook, or sometimes the man sharing her bed, come out to the well, and never at night. Other young men knock at the door, throw pebbles at windows, or write pleading or aggressive letters, with varying results. All this is an irritation she cannot live without.

One night, then, she dreams of a tribe of dogs. They are noble and speechless. She herself is a deer; she feels this arrangement of things, as you might expect, dangerous. The dog tribe mills about, paying little attention to her, but one of them sits and watches her, waiting, and she knows he is waiting for her to run. He has a blue stone in his skull. She feels an increasingly pressing desire to flee, though there is no good reason for it and good reason not to, with his eye upon her. She resists the impulse as long as she can, but knows there will come an end to her power to hold back.

When she starts to run, the dog yawns and begins to lope after her. Soon all the dogs are in chase, baying, and she is bounding away in great leaps, flying like a bird when she's in the air, but bound to pant and glance back behind her in fear, a four-legged beast, when her hooves touch the earth. She knows in the end she'll be caught, so at last she turns and stands.

The dog king stops. He walks up to her and drops his head so that the stone at the base of his skull shows. He has offered his neck, so she cuts it with her razor-sharp hooves. The stone, dislodged, rolls out on to the ground, and she takes it in her teeth. She swallows it. She is tired and lies down, waiting for the other dogs to kill her, but they merely circle her, panting, their teeth showing. She waits.

When Ariane awakes, she doesn't remember this dream. Her current lover, an inveterate reader of newspapers, tells her at breakfast that a strange plague has been reported in India, dogs and newts falling out of the sky. Ariane finds this difficult to believe but nonetheless feels disgruntled by his amusement with the story. She tells him he wastes his time, reading that newspaper all the time, and doing nothing, really, with his life, while she does all the actual work and suffers to boot. He says you could hardly call singing work, and soon the house is echoing with shouting, weeping, and the slamming of doors. As usual, there is a disheveled young man hanging around by the back garden that evening; the cook, cursing the heat, the useless sheriff's department, and lovers of music, drives him away.

Next, the dogs turn up in the western mountains, disguised as coyotes, or perhaps wolves, looking suspiciously mongrel and citified. The farmers in the valley are disturbed by the loss of calves and lambs and get out their guns and set traps. At night sometimes there's howling that doesn't have the singing, moon-inspired quality of wolf or coyote speech but instead that noisy bass thud of dogs barking at night. But before anybody can shoot one or verify the various sightings the dogs disappear. Two or three strays turn up in town, but that's not so unusual.

7.5

One night Nicanor wakes up with something very heavy lying on his chest. At first he thinks it's his death. But then, when his sight clears, he sees that it's a big - - - - creature. You and I know, a split second before he does, that it's a dog; he thinks at first it's a cloud of bad air combined with a dream or chili peppers, then god forbid an intruder, a thief or murderer about to kill him, then a dog. A black dog. While his actual and mental sight clears and he re-enters our story (his wife, who is asleep and remains asleep, stays in her own story) the dog, who is looking right into his eyes with his big black dog eyes, heaves himself up and jumps off the bed. The bed bounces and jerks as he leaves it. Nicanor is trying to catch his breath. He does not wake his wife because 1) he believes he is dreaming 2) if he is not dreaming he doesn't have time and must go straight on before it does become a dream through trying to explain it.

He sits up and puts his hand out in the dark bedroom. The dog puts its head under his palm and Nicanor feels, as you might expect, a round smooth patch at the base of his skull. He leans down and looks. He sees a blue stone, which in the dimness has its own blue light.

A feeling of confusion and at the same time tremendous clarity, like a light exploding all the objects in the room into substance, seizes him, and something exactly the size and weight of that stone turns over in his memory. This moment holds its shape perfectly, like an unburst bubble, till it passes. The next moment he hears the click of the animal's claws on the floor, and the dog jumps out the window. Nicanor rushes to the window; the last he sees of the dog is a dark shape galloping away in the moonlight without sound, already more like dream-shadow than a dog. He touches the back of his own skull and though he has no sensation there, certainly not one of pain, he feels as though he has received a wound, or a bite.

The next night he goes to bed hoping, strangely, for a visit from this dog, though the experience was not one you could call pleasant and he is not particularly a fancier of dogs, black or otherwise. He waits, unsleeping, while the night advances, and the house around him breathes in and out. He waits, and does not sleep. But he has no night visitors. Except the moonlight, which crawls along the floor with its accustomed strange and relentless beauty, a beauty that makes Nicanor wish now, as he has before, that moonlight itself could be a creature.

The Origin of Opera

Deep in the Indian Ocean live many mermaids. The Indian Ocean happens to be—this has been known since long before the sphinx roared for the last time—a very mer-ish place. However, though the female mer population is large, there are few mermen. No one knows why. The imbalance is ancient, though mysterious, and so the mermaids have become used to looking elsewhere for companionship of the amatory kind.

This is how they do it.

They go ashore. Though it is difficult, even painful, for mermaids to navigate in air and on sand, they have demanding traditions, and this is an adventure into a strange and uncivilized world—to them, the wild—they are driven to make.

At a certain time of year, they cluster. They follow each other toward the edge of their world. Near the place on the beach where they most often emerge, enterprising local merchants who know the habits of sea creatures of this binary kind set up a makeshift midnight market in saris and shawls. Out of the surf come the mermaids, rising like columns of whirling moonlight from the foam. Streaming with salt water and sea light, they stand up on their long scaled tails, teeter on to the wet sand, and wrap their lower extremities in the gorgeous and variegated colors of the saris the merchants sell them, in exchange for a kiss, a shell, a pearl or two. Only the greenish tips of their finial fins show at the hems of the garments, like little bound feet. Off they pitter and pat over the sand in tiny steps, hips undulating, toward the town and its streets and markets.

It is always night, and the lit cigarettes of the men who are watching the beach look like stars floating below the walls of the town. Up the beach the mermaids move slowly but inexorably, exuding an aphrodisiacal and somewhat fishy smell. Their magnificent female torsos are not entirely hidden under the saris. Their dark or blonde hair ripples down their backs or is bundled up on their heads in glorious piles by combs that any woman who happened to glimpse them would envy—though this last almost never happens. Women are at home asleep, or, if they are up and about, something makes them drift away from the beach and toward the hills at the hour the mermaids come out of the sea.

There are men who cannot resist the smell of fish. Foam and froth remind them. It is these men who come down to the shoreline. There they find drifting shadows—indescribably beautiful women mincing along the beach, and these women, who murmur and beckon and sing short snatches of the most popular current tunes, lead them back, as midnight approaches, toward the iridescent line of waves lipping the smooth beach. It's a tropical island scene, a whiff of paradise, with twosomes scattered here and there. Couples wander and fold into sand. Water creeps up the beach, sluices lightly over legs and wandering hands. Some men, touching smooth and slippery skin and damp hair, feel moments of fear, a horror of strangeness. They shiver. The mermaids stroke their hair, murmur soft seafoam words. Other men, to whom no second thoughts or questions occur, bend their heads toward stars and shells. A few pull away and walk quickly back up the beach, trying to spit out the taste of seaweed. But many a man holding a mermaid's hand feels that his life has arrowed down into the target of this very moment. His legs feel weak, and his desire is all to follow and find, to enter and shudder. Into the surf the mermaid and man step together and wind arms around each other. Hips, shoulders, the slide of rough skin. Slippery tongues and fingers. Down on to knees, falling into water, wetness and swelling everywhere, and soon the sari falls away. Now foam fills his mouth, her breasts press against him, and somehow he finds how to enter her, a twist or twinge and then heat, like entering a shadow or a pool when the sun has been too fierce, to find first a warm and then a cool current.

Some men who make love to mermaids drown in the act. They don't know whether they're coming or dying; then water fills their lungs. They're found the next morning, rolling naked in surf. Some survive, but at the encounter's height they feel as though their arms have been holding a scarf or a dolphin and have suddenly emptied, filled only with windy wet and half-shivered desire.

Mermaids are single-minded and voracious. They smell of sea and salt and the abyss. Once they have made love with these men, they flip their tails up, slap the water like whales and swim back into the deepest sea. There they wait for news from their bellies. The lucky ones will bear children. For that's the point of all this. Children. The combination of this and that to make the song continue.

Nine months later (for the gestation period is like ours), the lucky ones bear infants. Some of these are mergirls, a few merboys, and some look completely human, no tails or fins or scales, though they can breathe underwater and have, like all merpeople, irresistible singing voices.

When these children of the third kind are three or four—the age before which all memory is made up of ocean and shadow—their mothers take them back to the beach and explain that they belong to the land. See, they say, see, you have legs. The children see, for the first time, that they are different. Go. Explore the sand. Walk up the beach. You will find it pleasing. The children go, but their mothers are weeping, for mermaid mothers are like all others. The children walk out of the surf, looking back, unsure. The mothers, weeping, wave them on, and, wondering, they walk up the sand toward town. When they look back, the sea is still and flat. Their mothers are gone.

They sleep on the beach or wander into town and huddle in the corners of doorsteps. Most of these children are found the next morning by the people who live in the beachside town, and by one means or another they end up blended back into the land population, adopted into families, taken in somewhere as servants or inured to living by their wits, which are sharp, on the street.

They all have beautiful singing voices. They all smell of brine. Some of them get lost in other waters: tequila or music, sex, flamenco, thievery or dance. They all return, again and again, all their lives, to the beach, and they can swim like fish. (Surfers or marine biologists or great opera singers or the drunken lady who sits at the top of the marina steps with shells around her neck, boat-builders, weavers and astronomers surfing the interstellar oceans—who knows how they grow up or what they become.) But each fish child, at some time in his or her life, ends up at the beach one strange night, following an irresistible urge. Maybe the moon is full or the iridescent plankton are spread out on the water's belly. Maybe the water is filled with tires and stained with oil. Maybe the beach harbors people laughing and drinking beer down the way. Maybe it's entirely quiet, a moonlit night with only the suck and purl of water. Standing at the line of surf, this child of the sea hears a song that can only be a name. It is her name, or his. A name made of air and water, land and wet. And yearning. It's made up of the yearning of all creatures, no matter where they live—air, water, land, under the volcano or high up near the ice—to join, to know each other, the yearning for union with another not wrapped in the same skin.

After hearing that name, each of these people, these people who are whole in a way we almost wish to discover—understands the nature of doubleness, and from then on they know it: without being double or many you cannot be whole.

Fable with Wings

She was born with wings, but no knowledge of flying. Her parents never commented. Maybe they didn't notice, since at first the wings were more like nubs or odd bumps, and anyway, they were often too busy with the drama of the day's many logjams and potholes to notice much but each other's inadequacies.

When she herself noticed the wings, they seemed like sixth toes or something, useless appendages, though at least not as froggy as extra toes. At first she hid them. If she stood a certain way and dressed right, they seemed pretty much like large shoulder blades. Later, she wound beads and scarves in their feathers, tied them into a plume like a long pony tail, and made them into a fashion accessory.

Then, one high summer noon, she saw how free and light, how sweetly deep, that blue dome above her was. Maybe the wings actually worked. And well well, come to find out, they did. Her first few flights were careful: up into leaves, a bit of leaf muss and flurry, awkward bounce forward on to branches, teeter, and then an exultant perch on a branch, almost in the clouds it felt like, looking down with no fear.

On her next aerial adventure, practicing swoop-turns above a meadow, she encountered a large raven dangling some grapes above a fox's raised and drooling mouth.

"What are you doing?"

"Shh," said the raven, "I'm concentrating."

"Yeah, beat it," said the fox. "I've just about got him hypnotized."

Her first thought had been sympathetic to Fox—she'd always had a soft spot for those pointy noses and furry tails and of course that red—but, given this last remark, Raven's burnished black seemed no less striking, possibly even more attractive, than Fox's red.

Interesting, like the undetermined contest between ground and sky.

So she tried to hover. The problem was her starboard wing had a tendency to pull. This caused first a slow drift and then a faster veer, and abruptly she went into a spin, unfortunately in the moment's crisis flapping her arms instead of her wings. Blam, ruffle *thud*! as she careened into Raven, whose hover, she had time to notice before she bashed into him, was perfect. Most of the grape cluster, in the commotion, dropped into Fox's mouth, and, alert as always, he immediately swallowed both the grapes and Raven's foot. Raven squawked loudly, beat his wings frantically and actually managed to drag Fox, clamped on to his foot with grape-juice running down his jaw, upward off the ground. Fox looked down at friend Earth as it grew farther away beneath the glorious red of his tail, now tucked between his hind legs. Raven pumped his wings. "Grab her! Grab that... thing with the hair!" Raven squawked. "Grab her instead! She's bigger!"

Oh oh, she thought, thinking of those sharp little teeth, and accelerated when she should have braked, ending dangerously close to the melee. Fox opened his mouth and made a snap at her foot, which, being nimble in that department at least, she snatched back just in time. The sound of his teeth snapping in air lingered in her mind.

A thud, a most unfoxlike yowl, and Fox, now a reddish-brown heap on the ground, quickly metamorphosed into a ragged streak of iron oxide after-image that disappeared into a bush. There was a sound of whining from the greenery.

Raven flew up close to her and peered at her with his black, calculating eye. "Don't fly too well, girlie, do you? I offer lessons. Cheap."

The Mystery Writer

"All this is like a dream which the word bears within itself and which, passing through him who writes, is freed and frees him."
Italo Calvino, *The Castle of Crossed Destinies*

He did believe in certain verities. Principal among them the proposition that you could depend—a little more than provisionally, one could surely say—on the structural underpinnings of any communication. A certain devotion to the shared groundwork language provided. It boiled down to precision. Underscored by the social compact ensuring respect for a literate restraint on vague, ill-formed ideas and slipshod linguistic usages—usages which led both to messy intellectual habits and strained or misunderstood exchanges. Things in their place, for god's sake. So it was quite annoying when she kept referring to transformation so casually and—well, irresponsibly, really—as though it were a matter of olives to tangerines in the refrigerator or socks to gloves deep in some dresser drawer. As though everything had the ability to become something else, and the process was somehow both daily and, though largely un-noticed, central to existence.

"But look at day to night," she said. "Every day! Or I should say, to be precise, every 24 hours. Egg to chicken! Fog to ice!"

"To be precise," he muttered, "none of that is transformation. It's just organic chemistry, developmental growth, earth spinning on its axis."

"Of course!" Blithely. "But that's what transformation is. Natural!" Using, audibly, another damn exclamation point. How could you argue with these constant exclamation points and shifts of venue? It was tiring. His ears burned. He went off to his study.

The piece he was working on lay on his desk, and the words themselves drew him, as though their presence on the page had a mild magnetic force. He sat down and re-read what he had written in the morning.

The morning light moved slowly, inexorably, over the runkled surface of the blue sweater covering the man's broad back. He lay splayed across the lawn's rather putrid green, the stiff, short blades of the recently-cut grass pressed against one bulged cheek, while the other was, below the eye open and staring, too white.

A bit over-written. Too many clauses? "Rather" snagged him. Fussy. But runkled. He liked that: a made-up word, proving the birds of language could still fly in and dust up the territory in his head. Proving... something or other: that he was the same lineage as Shakespeare? that language itself had its own drive to colonize the human brain? that writing was still fun?

He was, after all, tired of constructing the endless puzzles mystery-writing required, weaving the threads, dropping the clues, obscuring the trail, unspooling the same story (but disguised) over and over again: of the ravaged orders of the world depicted and then bit by bit re-blocked into a sequence that provided proof of the investigative prowess of humans, our genius for solution, the small comforts of knowledge gained. He was tired of scaring people and then reassuring them. The excitements of nightmare. Of going into the darkness to... what? check the pulse of the monster that waited there and return to report that thinking still works to map the tunnel? if not to slay the beast itself...

He read it again. Still liked runkled. Though spell-check continued to try to correct it to "rankled." He took out "rather" and then put it back in. Considered the adjectives, felt suddenly tired. Decided to turn in.

He went to bed. So did she. No doubt they dreamed. If their dreams were similar, they did not know it. If they differed deeply, it would have surprised neither of them, though there had been, many years ago, occasions on which they had dreamed almost the same thing. He had forgotten this. She had not.

When he woke the next day, he did the usual things. Coffee, breakfast, walk. The paper, and then all the this-and-that that took so much time. Finally, he went to his study, with that little lift and tremor that always accompanied climbing the stairs. From the kitchen, she chimed: "Happy hunting!" So always cheerful, which was both a boon and a burden.

He sat down. Turned on his computer. As was his habit, he read over the print-out of what he had just written, with an eye to polishing before starting in on anything new. His habitual warm-up.

The light, pitiless and inexorable, moved slowly over the runkled surface of the blue sweater covering the man's broad back. He lay flayed on the lawn's rather putrid green, the sharp blades of the recently-cut grass prunting one cheek, while the other was, below the eye, an object without purpose for sight or anything else, too white.

He read it again. Surely that wasn't... wait a minute. "Runkled" was there, but so was "prunting," a word he knew he hadn't written, and one that seemed quite likely made-up. Yesterday? By him? And the rest of it, too, seemed changed. Hadn't he said "morning light?" and, yes, there was "pitiless and inexorable," but? – it didn't sound quite like what he'd written, and he knew he hadn't said that thing about the eye being an object. Wait a minute!

He scrabbled among his papers, looking for the earlier version. Nothing.

He opened the file on his lap-top. It read the same as the print-out.

Was he going nuts? It seemed quite clear that this wasn't what he had written originally, but now the whole thing seemed blurry. Maybe he'd written a number of versions and was remembering an earlier one? But no, that was a possible solution, an idea about what could have happened. It wasn't what actually had happened, because he hadn't written a number of versions. Had he?

Prunted? Where the hell did that come from? He looked it up. Prunt was actually a word, meaning little dollops of glass left on hand-blown glass. He hadn't known this before. He looked through the papers on his desk again. No other versions.

Sleep-walking? Some prank by his wife? Neither of these possibilities seemed at all likely. But after all, he was a mystery writer. Figuring out how things happened was his stock in trade. Well, figuring out how things happened in a story. Being a writer and being a detective are two different things. He'd always suspected that writing about this stuff involved more intellectual vigor and flexibility than actually solving crimes. This had been borne out in all the conversations he'd had with cops and investigators. Mostly their jobs didn't seem to involve either IQ or invention (in distinction to the detectives depicted in mysteries), and the detectives were often boring and bored: sitting around in cars squinting at motel entrances, checking data bases on a computer or slogging through dog-eared files in some un-airconditioned office in order to file endless reports regarding quotas, protocol and use of time, no mention of evidence or theories... He brought his mind back to the strangeness in front of him.

What the hell was going on? Though change is constant, that doesn't refer to the words on a page. They just stand there, forever the same, once you put them down. That was what made words both beautiful and treacherous. They waited there. Normally speaking. Inexorable. Pitiless. Spread out on the paper like a corpse on a lawn... no, no, this was nuts.

He went downstairs and into the kitchen. His wife wasn't there. The whole idea, anyway, of her playing a prank of this type on him was absurd. She would never do that. She was too kind, too earnest, to send him into a tizzy of this magnitude.

Not that there was really any magnitude to it. It must all be some kind of mistake or forgetfulness on his part. After so much futzing over what you wrote, it was easy to forget the particulars of the final revision. Wasn't it? Actually, no it wasn't, he answered himself. Not if you'd just written it the day before. You remembered. The words took their places. They danced to a certain tune. They didn't always behave as you wished, but they did stick on the page, like little limpets. They didn't go tromping off on their own, re-arranging themselves into another dance formation. They stuck around, sometimes causing a great deal of trouble because of their incontrovertibility, the way they continued—ad infinitum—to say what they said.

So what was going on here? How could this passage seem so different to him? He had had the experience of looking at words he'd written long ago and wondering how he'd ever managed to write that, even of forgetting the substance of what he'd written. But he'd never had the experience of looking at a piece of recently-written work and feeling that he had not written it at all, or that the writing was different than he remembered.

He went back upstairs but found he had developed a minor dread about re-reading the piece. He lingered close to his desk, hands on hips, pretending he was thinking about how to proceed.

Okay. He would just get on with the story. He could always change this beginning if it didn't suit... He sat down. He read it over. He began to type. It was slow work, but after a while, this is what he had.

The light, pitiless and inexorable, moved slowly over the runkled surface of the blue sweater covering the man's broad back. He lay flayed—okay, it shouldn't be flayed—he changed it back to splayed—*on the lawn's rather putrid green, the sharp blades of the recently-cut grass prunting one cheek, while the other was, below the eye an object without purpose for sight or anything else, too white.*

In his usual way, Eddie took his time, methodically scanning the body for details that stood out. He leaned down and lifted the man's left pant leg slightly. He took out his notebook and wrote down "knuckles" and, under that, "socks." The back of the man's head was bashed in; it was a crunched-in mess, hair and bone and blackish blood congealed at the base of the skull. His collar was dark with blood. One arm was flung up, the other lay down near the hip, and the legs looked as though he'd fallen in a running posture, in mid-stride. He was a muscular, short man. The knuckles on the flung-up left hand were bloody, as though he'd hit someone or something, and, though he was otherwise neatly, even elegantly dressed—gray slacks, blue sweater, the bit of collar left unbloodied showing a well-starched pin-stripe—his socks, above polished black shoes, were the wrong color. Brown. Maybe it was just an off laundry day. Maybe. Eddie snapped his notebook shut and went to look for Loden, who was in a particularly bad mood that day—in fact, since his wife had left him a month ago, this particular bad mood had pretty much become a perpetual state of mind, and Loden would probably tell him that any ideas he had about socks and knuckles sucked. So he just wouldn't mention it. 'Til after coffee.

That would do. It was at least three pages less than usual, but all he could manage today. He printed out two copies. Telling himself he wasn't really doing anything too out of the ordinary, and not completely willing to articulate the theory behind this move, he left one copy on his desk and took one downstairs, where he folded it and put it in a book on his night table.

That night, before he went to bed, he read it over. The words stood firm, in their habitual way. Nothing out of the ordinary there. And why should there be? Really. He said nothing to his wife about all this. It seemed—the all this, whatever it was—not something to dignify, exactly, with explanation and anxiety. Nonetheless, he couldn't ignore the fact that it took him longer than usual to go to sleep. Some word, something like inexorable but mixed up with both *runkled* and a new word that sort of plastered itself across his consciousness right before he went to sleep: *broidered*, both intrigued and bothered him, floating around behind his eyelids. Of course, he liked words. Of course. But this revisionary confusion, whatever it was and interesting as it might be, smacked of some vast practical joke or conspiracy he wasn't part of. He didn't like mish-moshes. He drifted off to sleep.

When he woke up, his stomach hurt and he had a mild sore throat—oh god maybe he was coming down with a cold? From somewhere nearby he heard the roar of a leaf-blower or some other annoying piece of equipment. His wife was already up; he heard water running in the kitchen. Right away he reached over for the book in which he'd inserted the print-out of his story. He pulled it out and read it sitting on the edge of the bed. God in heaven. Shit.

The light, broidered flecks of sun and shadow moved slowly over the runkled surface of the blue sweater covering the man's broad back. He lay loosened into stillness on the lawn's rather putrid green, the sharp blades of the recently-cut grass prunting one cheek, while the other was, below the eye an object without purpose for sight or anything else, too white.

As he always did, Eddie took his time, methodically scanning the body for details and clues. Things that didn't fit. Stuff that stuck out. Ah, the hands. With his pencil he lifted the man's left pant leg slightly. He took out his notebook and wrote down "knuckles" and, under that, "socks." The back of the man's head was bashed in, hair and bone and blackish blood congealed in an ugly mess at the base of the skull. A dark triangle of blood stained his collar. His left arm, flung up, seemed to be in the act of clutching something, and the knuckles on that hand were bloody, as though he'd hit someone or something; the other arm lay down near the hip, and the legs looked as though he'd fallen in mid-stride, running fast. He was a muscular man, short; even in death he looked bullishly strong. Though he was otherwise neatly, even elegantly dressed—gray slacks, blue sweater, the bit of collar left unbloodied showing a well-starched pin-stripe—his socks, above polished black shoes, were the wrong color. Brown. Maybe it was just an off laundry day. Maybe.

Eddie snapped his notebook shut and went to look for his partner Loden, who was in a particularly bad mood that day—in fact, since his wife had left him a month ago, after telling him she never wanted to see him again in this *world or any other, this particular bad mood had pretty much become a perpetual state of mind—and it was a good bet Loden would probably tell him that any ideas he had about socks and knuckles sucked six ways to Friday. So he just wouldn't mention it. 'Til after coffee.*

Jesus. He sat there. He read it again. It was changed. He knew it was changed. He ran upstairs, not even bothering, as he passed the kitchen door, to explain this oddity in his morning routine. As he took the stairs, he registered the faraway but definite cough of the leaf-blower growing louder. He grabbed the other copy off his desk. Of course. It was the same as the one downstairs.

He read it again. Surely this version was different than what he had written yesterday. The broidered flecks of shadow started it off. Broidered. He'd never used that word. Even heard of it, though some shred of dream-memory made it seem familiar. And then the rest of it. Loosened into stillness. Lifted with his pencil. Dark triangle. Bullishly. Bullishly? This world or any other. Six ways to Friday. He hadn't written that stuff. He was sure. And that was only part of it. The rest of it seemed subtly changed, too.

And the worst thing of all was that it was better. It seemed. Although how could he tell, really? He couldn't be sure of the relative merits of the versions without, for god's sake, the earlier version, but it was as though he had revised it and improved it. But he hadn't. He hadn't.

Next door the bluster of the motor grew louder, an interfering noise that settled in his shoulders.

Calm down, he told himself. There's an explanation for this. But his mind ricocheted off its own walls, finding no explanation. "Be right down," he shouted to his wife, and then, having nothing better to do and having said he would do it, he went downstairs. He couldn't decide whether to leave the paper clutched in his hand on his desk. He crumpled it up and put it in the pocket of his bathrobe, where, all during breakfast, he could not forget it. He wanted to tell his wife about it, but he couldn't think of how to do it. It sounded too nuts. If only he could prove it. If only he could somehow save these various versions and show how they'd changed...of course then they'd simply look like regular revisions, nothing odd about them. Even though he hadn't actually written them.

Early Alzheimer's?

A sudden silence as the noise of the motor next door ceased. Clearly, it wasn't a leaf blower. That idiot must be doing another renovation.

"Christ," he said. "He's at it again."

"Is that why you're frowning like that, Carl? You look pretty upset."

"No, no, it's... something I'm working on... bit of a puzzle."

"Oh? Something difficult?" She buttered a piece of toast, smiled. The noise started up again.

"Well, one of those snags. Where things aren't going as you planned, and you don't really know where the story's off to—" He squeezed his eyes shut. Really, that noise...

"Ah. I thought that was what made it fun. The muse, etc. The feeling you're not in control."

"Well, yeah. Sometimes. But this... I can't quite get the story to go my way, or something. It's so easy to get side-tracked, and then you have to throw it all out later."

"Well, don't worry. I'm sure you'll work it out. You always do."

He grunted and finished his coffee. How could you work something like this out?

For the next few days he was driven practically to distraction by the noise in his neighbor's backyard. His neighbor—a retired guy named Gus Morales—whose house projects had been pretty much constant, as well as noisy, since Carl and his wife had moved in, had taken it into his idiot head, it seemed, to build a pool in his backyard. It became quickly clear that this involved large equipment, digging, pouring a great deal of concrete, and more or less constant comings and goings by a large crew of workers who set up boomboxes in the backyard and parked large, ramshackle trucks in front of the house. For god's sake, the man was well into his 60's: why did he need a pool? Couldn't he just join a gym?

Carl had had a number of conversations with this guy, who lived alone in an ever-expanding house. Conversations about the need for quiet in the neighborhood in general, and in his own vicinity in particular. He'd explained about being a writer. About working at home. Gus had smiled affably and said he understood. However, he also said that now he was retired, he had time to indulge his own creativity, which involved his house. Architecture had always been a second love. The first being bread—he had had a bread-baking business which had apparently done quite well. At the end of each project he delivered a bottle of good wine and a loaf of excellent bread to their door. This did not make up for the noise, the dust, the discombobulation.

One fortunate side-effect of the current distraction, however, was that the whole stream of odd occurrences with the writing came to a halt. Carl hadn't written a word in three days. Hadn't even gone into his study. At night he'd done a bit of planning and note-taking, that's all. He refused to admit to himself that this was a relief, and that Gus's current project had come at a time he really couldn't wholeheartedly call inconvenient. Nonetheless, he continued to complain to Ginny, who agreed (despite her penchant for viewing everything from an annoyingly positive point of view) that the noise made life at home not quite the stress-free and quiet retreat they'd both envisioned when they'd moved to this quiet side-street in a leafy neighborhood.

On Thursday morning, the fourth day, Carl marched up to his study, determined, despite any disturbance, to get going again on the new project. He sat down at his desk and glanced out the window. The view gave on his neighbor's back yard, where a large, muddy-looking hole, random piles of rock and brick, and a number of concrete mounds with rebar sticking out of them disfigured the landscape. To his surprise, there was his wife, standing next to the barely-imagined pool, talking to Gus. They stood face-to-face and fairly close, and Ginny was gesturing vigorously. Gus leaned in toward her and put one hand on her shoulder. Then he patted her. And Ginny laughed. At least that's what it looked like. She bent over, holding her stomach. Either she was being sick or she was laughing quite hard. And Gus was grinning, standing there with his hands on his hips. He looked quite pleased. Carl noticed for the first time that, despite his shock of white hair and rather big nose, Gus was quite good-looking for his age.

What was going on?

He wanted to rap on the window. He felt he should turn away. After all, they were just having a joke. Ginny stood up, still laughing. She waved—was that a kiss, for god's sake, she blew in Gus's direction?—and walked away out of sight, presumably back toward their own house.

Carl sat still, staring out the window. His neighbor was standing by the putative swimming pool, hands on hips, staring down into the empty space. Perhaps he was imagining water, seeing aquamarine and flecks of sunlight. Carl certainly respected imagination—after all it was his stock in trade. Backyard pools, though, were merely attractive nuisances and ecological energy sucks. Maybe he could weave something featuring drowning or concrete into the current story? A guy goes out to check some noise in his backyard at night, falls into the excavation for his pool and breaks his neck? Or so it seems, because later it transpires he's been lured out by the sound of his wife laughing loudly... His mind wandered. His throat hurt. Somewhere back there he had heard the back screen-door slam. Now Gus was talking to a guy, probably the contractor, since he was dressed in a leather jacket and carried no tools. The sound of a jack-hammer began. Carl squeezed his eyes shut. Okay. Down to work, damn it.

The light, broidered flecks of sun and shadow moved slowly over the runkled surface of the blue sweater covering the man's broad back. He lay loosened into stillness on the lawn's rather putrid green, the sharp blades of the recently-cut grass prunting one cheek, while the other was, below the eye, an object without purpose for sight or anything else, too white.

As he always did, Eddie took his time, methodically scanning the body for details and clues. Things that didn't fit. Snagged your eye. Made you wonder. The back of the man's head was bashed in, hair and bone and blackish blood congealed in an ugly mess at the base of the skull. A dark triangle of blood stained his collar. His left arm, flung up, seemed to be in the act of clutching something, and the knuckles on that hand were bloody, as though he'd hit someone or something. The other arm lay down near the hip, and the legs looked as though he'd fallen in in mid-stride, running fast. He was a muscular man, short; even in death he looked bullishly strong. With his pencil Eddie lifted the man's left pant leg slightly. He took out his notebook and wrote down "socks," and, under that "knuckles." Though the corpse was otherwise neatly, even elegantly dressed—gray slacks, blue sweater, the bit of collar left unbloodied showing a well-starched pin-stripe—the man's socks, above polished black shoes, were the wrong color. Brown. Maybe it was just an off-laundry day. Maybe.

Eddie snapped his notebook shut and went to look for his partner Loden, who was in a particularly bad mood that day—in fact, since his wife had left him a month ago, after telling him she never wanted to see him again in this world or any other, this particular bad mood had pretty much become a perpetual state of mind—and it was a good bet Loden would probably tell him that any ideas he had about socks and knuckles sucked six ways to Friday. So he just wouldn't mention it. 'Til after coffee.

Thank god, nothing seemed to be changed. No jarring made-up words or images slyly kaleidoscoped into a different coloration. But wait—somehow the word corpse jumped out at him. And wasn't there a subtle shift, something with the sequence? He put his head in his hands. Nothing to compare it with, and now he didn't entirely trust his memory and wished... what? that the story had been tattooed on his arm, like his grandfather's death-camp tattoo, where he could read it in all its skin-blazoned, time-stopped and brutal verity? He shook his head, as though to dislodge water or get rid of some blur. It was more than he wished to think about.

Okay. He focused on the last words he'd written—after all, they were his words—and launched himself into the waiting blankness. After a while, he began to feel a flow.

Loden was talking to the woman in the house, who claimed the man lying on her back lawn was a complete stranger to her, and since the corpse had no identification on his person, there was no way to check this out. Mussed-looking, still dressed in a blue cotton bathrobe, she was sitting at a wooden kitchen table, her blondish hair pushed behind her ears in a tangled puff, and she was visibly trembling, as though cold. She didn't look up when Eddie came in. She held one hand over her mouth.

Eddie took a quick survey of the kitchen. Neat. White tile counters with enough kitchen appliances to suggest an interest in fancy cooking. Vase of sunflowers on the end of one counter. Dirty dishes in the sink, beside which stood two wineglasses, one half full of red wine. There was a dog dish on the floor at the end of one counter, but no dog in evidence.

Loden was speaking in his most soothing voice. "Okay. This is quite a shock, I know. Is there someone you could call to come be with you?" The woman said something unintelligible from behind her hand.

"What?" said Eddie.

"Of course, of course," said Loden, "but we need as much information as possible about last night, obviously. I do have a few more questions, and my partner may have a few, too." He gestured toward Eddie. "This is my partner, Eddie Louisiana. Madeleine Towers, the owner of the house."

"How do you do, Mrs?—" Eddie paused interrogatively—"Towers—"

"Louisiana?" The woman looked up at him, ignoring his implied question. "Your name is Louisiana?"

"It is," said Eddie. He was used to this kind of question, and tried to be polite about it.

"Well. Hunh." She laughed once, a barking cough. "I suppose it's better than being called Mississippi. Or Texas."

"Agreed. Though harder to spell. People get it wrong all the time." He smiled.

"So. Can you tell us if you heard anything last night?"

She shook her head. "Nothing. I already told him."

"If I may ask, do you sleep soundly? Take sleeping pills?" Her face looked bleary to him. He wondered if she drank.

"As a matter of fact, I sleep quite lightly." She had stopped trembling, and this remark was made in a slightly

truculent tone, as though Eddie were trespassing in a forbidden
personal zone.

"Did your dog wake up?"

"What dog?"

Eddie gestured toward the dog dish. "Don't you have—?"

"No. I don't. My neighbor comes over often, and I keep
that out for her dog."

"Ah." Eddie made a note. "What time did you get up,
and when did you go into the garden?"

"All these questions." She sighed. "About 8:00. I went to
bed rather late last night, actually, so I was late getting up. I took
my coffee into the garden about 8:30."

Carl went back up to the beginning of the piece and added
something about a coffee cup dropped on the lawn, spilled
coffee. The noise next door, which had seemed to recede
as he concentrated, lurched into the foreground again. The
question, which he had been pushing to the back of his
mind, about what Ginny and Gus had been talking about,
took hold, interfering with his concentration on the story.
He decided to take a break.

Downstairs, he poured himself some coffee and
wandered into the living room, where he stood staring
out the window at a large white truck marked PROMPT
PLUMBING—24 HOUR SERVICE parked in front of
the house. The noise of a generator burred dimly in the
background. Suddenly a thought came to him. He ran
upstairs as fast as he could without spilling his coffee. He

brought up the page he'd been working on. As he stood in front of his desk, leaning on his hands, staring at the screen with some vague idea of an electronic dubbuk (I.B. Singer) or a string theory parallel universe out of William Gibson (Kafka?), he realized he was panting. His own breath came and went like wind from another planet.

But the page was just as he'd left it, the words and letters marching along in polite files and parades under his mild command. Though relief flooded him at once, he noticed a slight blip of disappointment. No mysterious change. No magic. Or what the uninformed would call magic. And this little piece of detective work had failed to provide any clues. Okay. Down to work again. Quit running around.

"Please forgive all the questions. I know it can be annoying at such a time, but we do need to detail the circumstances, obviously. Do you live here alone, Ms. Towers?"

"I do." She looked up sharply, frowned.

"Did you have any visitors yesterday? Someone for dinner?" He glanced at the two wine glasses next to the sink, letting her notice.

She stared up at him. "No. Why do you ask?"

"Well, there are the two glasses."

"I did have a glass of wine with dinner, but the first bottle I opened wasn't good, so I poured some from a new bottle. Into another glass."

"Ah." He looked down at her, making his look deliberately neutral. In detective work it didn't pay to be too friendly, or, on the other hand, excessively skeptical. "Are you missing anything in the house? Anything out of place?"

She started rubbing her eyes again, and then, oddly, knocked the heel of her hand against one ear as though trying to dislodge water or kickstart a hearing apparatus. "Nothing I've noticed, but actually I haven't had much of a chance, not to put too fine a point on it, officer, to look around. Obviously. Excuse me. My ear is bothering me."

Eddie turned to Loden, giving her time to stop seething. "Anything from the neighboring houses?"

Loden shrugged. "The neighbor on the north side, a Mr. Brinkman, says he heard a loud cat-fight in the middle of the night. Woke him up. No one else heard anything."

"Did you hear something like that, Ma'am?" In some cases, calling them ma'am helped.

"No, I did not." Apparently this wasn't one of those cases.

"Okay. We're going to be taking pictures, moving the body, and checking your backyard and the neighbors' yards. We'll need to look around your house, too, if you don't mind."

She stood up. "I've got to get dressed." And off she marched.

"Woo," said Loden. "She's a bit of a bee–"

"–yatch? Yeah. But finding a dead fella in your backyard's kind of a rough way to start the day. Doesn't go well with the breakfast burrito."

"True. But being a bitch... that's maybe not due to..." His voice trailed off.

Eddie sighed and walked over to the counter, took out his handkerchief, and using it to pick up the glass, took a sip of the wine in the half-full glass. Loden raised his eyebrow.

"Perfectly okay, far as I can tell," said Eddie. "C'mon, coffee time, while the crime guys get down to business."

They discussed the corpse, the details, Madeleine Towers and her annoyed behavior and suspicious explanation of the two glasses. Loden dismissed the brown socks. "Trivial. Let's not get hung up on red herrings here." The bloodied hand, now, that was something. But what kind of something? Obviously the deceased had had a run-in with something solid, maybe someone's face. The crime scene guys would look for skin or signs of a solid object his fist had smashed into. He and Loden sent in a description of the body, which had no identification or money or weapon on it, and asked for info. on burglaries, disturbances reported in the neighborhood, missing persons. The crime scene guys finished, and the city hauled the body away.

"Well, that's pretty much that." Loden shoved his notebook in the sagging pocket of his jacket. Loden was looking unkempt these days, Eddie thought, but he didn't comment; instead he squinted at him as though in surprise. "Huh? Pretty much that? We're knee-deep here."

"Oh, I just mean we're done with Madeleine Towers and her back yard. Don't be so finicky."

But that, it turned out, was definitely not that.

Because the next day there was another corpse in Madeleine Towers' back yard.

Same approximate place, another un-nerving apparition pitched forward on to the lawn among flowers. Same shocking breakfast-time appearance with no apparent commotion during the night. This time the guy was thin and dressed like a flamenco dancer or a toreador. Some kind of clown suit, in other words. Head also bashed in. No identification.

Madeleine Towers was pretty much a wreck. And Eddie did have to admit that her back yard seemed to be developing fast into a very undesirable stop on a very treacherous route.

Carl decided to knock off for the day. Where the hell was this going, anyway? He knew he should probably follow this unexpected and unplanned turn in the story—a feature of writing he was familiar with—a little farther down the trail to see if it led into an impenetrable jungle or was actually one of the roads that led toward Rome, but he felt irritated by the toreador's injection of himself into the story—not a development that accorded with the plan he'd been developing so far—and he didn't feel like dealing with it right now. Maybe it would give him an interesting place to start tomorrow. If all went well, and the story didn't... he kept the thought fuzzy.

While he'd been writing, he'd been able to forget any questions about how to save the story, about wandering words, about mental dysfunction or maverick universes. But now that he was about to close down, he felt hot and his stomach hurt. Fear. Mixed with a tiny amount of curiosity, as though he had been chosen for alien abduction or a journey to an event threshold no one had ever described. Not that he believed in that kind of thing, of course, being a rational person. This whole confabulation with the words and the weird revisions was ridiculous—and yet it was happening. Wasn't it? Before he closed the file he sent a copy to his own phone and another to his wife's e-mail, and he printed out two copies. Then he saved and closed the file and sat staring at his computer screen, sweating, his stomach in knots. He opened the file again. Nothing had changed. It was all as he had just written it.

He thought about writing out a longhand version of the story, but rejected it as too time-consuming.

The real problem was that now he didn't know whether he was pleased at the words' compliance with normal reality, or not. He wasn't sure whether he wanted the phenomenon to disappear or remain. He was, he had to admit it, intrigued. And at the same time fearful of finding the words changed when he returned to work. So what did he want: the mystery of the wandering words, language grown nomad, or the normal steadfastness of written text, where an almost immortal solidity attached itself to these odd hatchmarks on a page? It was as though these written words had taken on the characteristics of oral expression, sliding, shifting, changing in each iteration, morphing, in memory, into alternate patterns, tripping two listeners up by bifurcating into two versions, both heard with absolute clarity, and remembered with complete confidence. Except these were *written* words. Ink, code, memory chips. Not memories of words. *Markings*.

He knocked his left ear with his palm, as though to shake out water. Whether he wanted this to be happening or not, it had. There had to be a rational explanation. A crack in the universe wasn't a plausible theory. Go lie down, he told himself. Take a walk. But he didn't. After all, the world is a very strange place, he thought, staring into the space above his desk. Brutal bloom, unexplained until it's explained, everywhere. Glowing sea creatures more like incandescent balloons than our idea of solid bodies. Transparent frogs. Time that bends.

He went downstairs. At the bottom of the stairs he paused. The house was eerily quiet. Yet in that silence he felt the seething of the world's presence, as though this anomaly had made him conscious once again, as he had been in childhood, of the complex magic of the actual world in all its unauthorized splendor, its gritty foreverness—where forests gave way to artic snow or desert sands just as barren as the moon, and mollusks and zebras and redwood trees were ancient kin. Standing there he felt inside him again some set of organic, irresistible rules of order and longing that bent and bloomed and blistered his life and all its aimings into both beauty and pain, how things always and even now in the festers of his middle life were dressed in the sleeves of the visible and invisible, like magnetism known and felt by migrating birds as well as iron filings and all the rest of it ratcheted right down to him and the palpable winds of an always-un-named joke and rule (his mother's ability to read his intentions, his father's weird hook into air to catch a ball, how birds fell out of the sky into just the right place without stumble, how on the long-ago school bus the cluster of his friends in one place made geography a matter of felt warmth) and now how his wife's face, when he saw her, brought a breath of ease into some clenched place inside him, how the universe read him (yes, *read*, he thought, that's the word) this knowledge through all his pores. Though not in words. As a child, none of it had been in words. In skin, in some watery tide inside him. In the steps he took, wherever they led him. And now, as an adult who trafficked in words, he knew they were, though immensely attractive, entirely unavailable to translate this—though that's what it was, writing, an attempt to translate that very thing.

He stood there. And then it was gone. A moment he remembered, but could not re-capture. He went and found his wife's sewing basket and took out a spool of gray thread, climbed back up to his office and stretched the thread across the doorway to his study about a foot up from the floor, securing it with two pushpins. He stood looking down at it, frowning. He had a divided mind, he realized. It was divided between hope and dread, and the trip wire was set right between those two poles.

At dinner he said to his wife, "So what were you talking to Gus about the other day? I saw you laughing. Standing next to the pool. The someday pool, that is."

"Oh." She smiled. "Actually, we were talking about you."

He frowned. "So what was so funny?"

She put her fork and knife down. "Carl, I wasn't laughing at you. It started with Gus saying that he was sorry for the uproar, but creativity, or change or something, always involved commotion." She waved her hands around in the air, displaying commotion. "And he was the kind of person who required a lot of mess to think something was actually happening. So I said that was just the wrong conditions for you, actually. Because that's what I'd gone over there to tell him. And he said, well, he was sorry, but he was sure that being mussed up by something would in the long run contribute to your work. And I said..."

"Ginny, this doesn't actually sound funny at all."

"Wait, wait, Carl. So I said, 'not really, Gus, it just makes him crazy' and he said well, crazy is the way the world works, he must know that if he's a writer, and then he said this kind of smart thing—"

"Yes?"

"—he said, 'it's the oyster and the pearl: annoy the artist and out comes something beautiful, something layered in effort. Right? Of course the artist suffers. Soft tissue. Abrasion. You know.' 'Gus!' I said, 'Pearls! You've certainly made a good case for mess. Mess and abrasion and, and..."

"'Concrete!'" he practically yelled, Carl, 'concrete! and next-door neighbors!'—it was pretty funny— 'He just doesn't know how lucky he is, living next to me! The creative annoyance of it all!' Or something like that. I tried to remind him. 'It all comes back, really, to noise... because he's trying to work...'

"'No, no' he said, 'it all comes back to pearls! And swine! That's me—I provide the crap!' Pointing at himself. 'Believe me, I'm indispensable.' And so we laughed! I mean he was being funny, Carl, you have to admit. He meant well. Really, he was making silk from a sow's ear right then and there. Always a good move." And she grinned. "He's really kind of an interesting guy, you know."

Carl looked at her. And although it wasn't really funny and it wasn't like the flood of un-named but momentous feelings he'd had at the bottom of the stairs, he recognized it. A creative effort. It was somehow a comfort, that she had tried to go to battle in his behalf, and now, too, this flow of words that tried, so energetically, to connect with what had made it funny at the time.

In the middle of the night he woke. He got out of bed and went upstairs. At the door to his study he stopped. He put his hand down to feel. The thread was still there.

He stepped over it, went in, turned on the light, checked the story.

It was just as he'd left it. No changes, no nagging sense of something vaguely drifting. No improvements. No wander.

In the morning, nothing was different.

The words never changed like that again.

He looked down at Gus's pool, glittering in the sun. Little flecks of light moving, almost in Brownian motion, against that aqua blue you see almost nowhere but in chlorinated water on a bright day. The pool had finally appeared a few months ago. Now invisible, but still a hologram that hovered, was the little landscape that had been there before, the lawn, and then the messy excavation, with all its attendant bother and noise. Though all this was still present in his memory. Or would be for a while, a fading image. His wife was right, of course. Transformation was constant. And mysterious.

Which was, as he'd always known, the problem with words.

On his desk, the finished manuscript lay in a neat stack. Inside that unremarkable rectangle, murder and mayhem and mystery laid bare. All words. Words. And though it was abundantly clear to him, by this time in his life, that mystery cannot be laid bare, in some ways the words flung themselves at it, meteors sharing a little something with the sun. He wondered, staring down at the manuscript, if now that it was done, the words would agree to stay loyally in their appointed places, obedient soldiers, or once again fling wide the doors to chaos and march out to their own tune.

Of course it was, somehow, his tune. Or so it seemed, because now the whole episode seemed itself like a story he had told himself, an invisible landscape buried under the present aspect of things.

His grand-daughter tapped him on the arm. He turned from his desk. "I'm going to be a writer too, Grandpa." She looked up at him with her greenish eyes.

"Oh?"

"Once the wind blew me down a hill. My feet went up off the ground—it was like flying. So I decided to write a story about riding the wind."

"Good plot. Could I see it?"

"I haven't written it yet."

"Ah." He lifted her up and set her on his lap, in front of his laptop. "Something kind of like that once happened to me. I was writing a story, but every night when I went to bed the words changed themselves. I'd get up in the morning, and they'd be different."

"Really?"

"Seemed like it. Don't know, really. It was a long time ago, but I don't think I'm making it up."

"Every night?"

"Every night. Well, for a while. Then it stopped. To tell you the truth, I was kind of disappointed." She stared, and for a moment his mind filled with a picture of their words flying like birds between them, clustering, settling, disappearing into the clouds and mountains that made up what they were to each other. "But once stuff is made," she said, "it lives somewhere, and then it looks like all the things around it."

"What do you mean?"

His grand-daughter didn't answer, looked aside, out the window. He waited. She tapped the desk, punched a key on his laptop.

"Don't do that." He shifted his knees, which hurt a bit.

"Did it ever happen again?"

"No."

"Maybe you made it up."

"Or maybe—" he smiled—"the words were playing a trick on me. They do that, you know."

She grinned. "Grandpa, what's the difference between a story and a lie?"

"A story, honey, reveals the truth. A lie disguises it."

"Do you know how to lie, too?"

He grinned. "Oh yeah. We all do."

She didn't smile, but her eyebrows arched in that way she had when she was hiding how pleased she was about something. "Let's write a story, then, that's all lies but tells the truth."

"Whowee," he said. "Maybe you will be a writer."

He never told anyone else about it.

Descent in Five Motions

Door

She sat up. Had there been a noise? The bedroom was dark, except for the pencil-thin line of light around the blind, cast by the streetlight. The cat's weight against her foot didn't shift. Had it been a door opening? She listened. Nothing.

Okay.

Carefully, not to disturb the cat, she folded back the covers and rose, feeling a bit dizzy. The floor felt furry, as though still made of dream molecules. She turned right at the bottom of the bed and followed a familiar pathway across the rug toward the unlit bathroom. Felt for the door, entered. Felt for the toilet seat. Cool air against her waving hand. Stepped forward. Stepped forward again. Again. She stopped. Steps at her feet, just visible now in the darkness, leading downward.

A cool wind from below.

Without hesitation, knowing she didn't know where she was, she started down. Thinking *is this a beginning, or an end?* And then she felt, at her feet, the cat. He was coming, too.

Nether

It was a dark and stormy noon. Lightning struck the front door. It flamed and crumbled to ash. In he walked. He towered, he stuck out his lower lip, he reached out a surprisingly small hand with gilt fingertips. His blond pompadour obscured his eyes.

—You're going to love me. I know everything about you. Which is your deepest crevice?—

Breathing seemed the best option, despite the stench. It had been years since she'd eaten a pomegranate, but she remembered the taste, red as blood.

—Come over here.— She patted the couch and smiled, demure curve. Behind the couch (it had been there a long time) was the stairway down. She'd kept her kids from going back there, but now...

He sat down, grinning, and reached for her right breast with his gilded hand. The cat ran behind the couch.

—Wait. Follow me! I know a better place.—

And she rounded the couch, just shy of his plucking hand, and ran down the dark stairway. *No stumbles,* she ordered her feet, *no stumbles. Ruthless, quick.* (Whose words were that?) He panted behind her, surprisingly agile despite his daunting size. Some mutter, then the roar: *do you know who I AM?* Gravel, a dark wind against her face. She would shut the door as he rushed past; she saw it ahead now. And then. She'd call the guard, the one with three heads (one head understood forest maneuver, one counted circles of hell, and the third had mapped the maze at the center of the earth). She remembered his name still: Caliban. Though half-covered in bark and tattooed by scorn and history's ugliness, this guardian was faithful to light.

She ran, at each step a seed sprouting.

Show Them Who's What

He steps (should he be running, sweeping, waving?) through a door. Feeling not quite like himself. More like someone too far from lunch, more like the paste he'd always eaten in third grade. He could remember that kid he'd tried to throw out the window, but he had no idea if he'd liked eating paste too. Probably not. He was a loser.

Anyway, soon as he gets through the door, a red carpet appears, as promised. But it branches, or whatever you call it when the map turns into a math equation. Crap. Too many exits and entrances. Too many signs with no neon and too many words. Boring. Also a little scary. Just go ahead and grab that...

He pictures a couple of her melons, plump under his...

Okay. There. That guy, the rumpled but smart one, waving him over there. So he goes. Over there. The roaring and applause convince him. Though for crapssake, it's all more than you could expect anyone who knows how to run something and be in charge I can tell you that believe me would pay attention to. He smiles at a guy in the back row. They love me. But the path squirms like a snake under his feet. Holy shit. Maybe that white thing is a golf ball?

He exits to the right. Couldn't have been a golf ball. Oh no! Could it have been one of those miniature drone-bomb things they keep telling him about? He scowls. Let's get things back on track, ok?—gilt-bargain signposts shining bright and also a fuckin' hamburger for crapssake.

Good time, that's it, to pick up the phone. Wait— tropical or tundra? World class hotel on an iceberg, penguin dinners. Great idea. Look at them out there, all waving banners and hats. You're beautiful people! The rumpled guy nodded and gleamed (somewhere back there; someone else is yammering at him now). So true. When you know what you're doing, you do it. Don't wait. Which means fire that little rat-faced guy who locked himself in the closet, didn't come through. Fire his ass.

He raises his right arm. The air told him to wave. Obviously, it approves.

The red carpet is looking navy blue. Or is it getting dark? Downward into the shadow is not his preferred direction, but the gravel makes it a bit slippery. Hard to stop.

Far off to the left is a low burr, maybe a growl. Something white, maybe a bird or model airplane, flies at him, lands at his feet. Ah crap. He sees what it is. He frowns. Then grins. No problem! He tears up the newspaper, balls it up, squeezes hard, looks at the bits and pieces of words in his hand. Sort of like burned French fries with mayo. He eats the clump. When it comes out the other end, it'll be digested. Then he'll post it.

Far off to the left, grumble seethes. He glances over. A shadow, of a massive female figure with one arm thrust into the air. A feeble light flickers in her hand. He ignores her—after all, she's needed serious reconstruction for a long time, and she can't walk. Okay. Let's move along here. He thinks of the noble sound the helicopter makes when he lifts off, eating a burger. The furry static buzzing on the horizon doesn't matter, probably just a fake sound effect anyway. His motto has always been: what you don't know should move to Sweden.

Memory of the Future

He sat in a gilt chair. His chariot had stalled in a rancid fog, which reduced visibility to twenty feet.

—Tule fog, he shouted. It will clear in a minute! If it doesn't, we'll sue!—

But particles of soot rained from a black sky, and the coal tar in our nostrils, along with the stench, made it hard to breathe.

—Do you like my helmet?— His smile showed a flash of dagger tooth.

—*Yes! Yes! Yes!*— the crowd shouted in unison. Four or five people collapsed from the effort.

—Do you like my scepter? I just love it!— He lifted his golf club.

More affirmative shouting. The crowd stood on the prone bodies of the people who had collapsed, gasping like beached fish, beneath the trample.

—Do you like my cabinet?— He opened a box on the seat next to him. Inside were three small figures about the size of Punch and Judy marionettes, two men and a woman. One, a gray-haired man in rumpled clothes, looked up and grinned. He raised a blunt-nosed handgun and pulled the trigger. *Bang!* Out shot a white flag with the words "Heil It!" into the air.

The crowd roared. Right hands soared upward into a forest of fingers.

The second man, in a dark suit, didn't smile or move. He was sitting on a large pile of money. He stared at a phone in his left hand, frowning. In his right hand he held a crumpled newspaper. Or was that a ball of caramel corn?

The third little puppet, the woman, was blonde in the same way platinum and yellow diamonds are blond. In fact, maybe her hair was made of Rumplestilskin's pale promise. (Where the needle was no one knew, though some might have looked at her shoes.) She was dressed in a white dress trimmed with crystals, and her belt was rust. She smiled and stepped out of the cabinet in her four-inch heels on to his lap, careful to miss the places that might cause pain or some kind of enlightenment. She nestled in, smiling a kewpie grin.

Everyone cheered. She waved and held up a contract in Chinese.

In the distance, you could hear the moan of ice, the roar of fires, the long howl of a wolf. The trees said words they had reserved for warning. The sky ached a certain gray. Minerva, in the form of an owl, entered stage left. She flew low and in utter silence over him, over the crowd, and out of the picture.

Now

I sit up in bed.
Middle of a dark night stretched into worlds.
Broom of virus sweeping. Falling towers.
Green seeping into air's tornado.
How many seeds have we eaten?
Is there a door?

Hair

A long time ago, and you're probably going to find this hard to believe, women—and men, too, though this probably wasn't important—were bald. Bald, you will say! How awful! Do you mean *bald* bald? Yes, I do. Bald as a rock, bald as an egg, bald as the dirt patch in the backyard where the chickens like to roam. Bald as a ringing gong, and just as beautiful, though of course this baldness was silent.

This was in a time before mirrors, and Lilith, whose ancestry we will not tabulate here, since it causes so much ruckus, was bald, too. As a bat. Though bats do have a hair or two sticking out. Lilith had one or two, too. This did not bother her, or cause plucking and primping, since there were no mirrors, and the occasional glimpse she caught of herself in pools or puddles only confirmed the impression she had gotten from the behavior of others, which was that she looked fine, perhaps more than fine, even though her skull might bounce light back like a billiard ball. (A class of balls which hadn't been invented yet, by the way.)

One day like other days, for they came in a stream, just like now but more so, a sameness and repetition that made it difficult to say this was that or brown was beige or corn was sugar or any of the other things people like to say to show that they can distinguish one thing from another quite well thank you, the sun came up. Big and round, golden. Bald, as you may have noticed. (Baldness is a much more pervasive quality than at first appears.) On this day Lilith had decided to visit her three children by her first husband, Adam. I hate to mention this, as you might begin to think I've got a bee in my bonnet (whatever that means), but her children—two sons and a daughter—were also bald. No one cared. Really.

What I mean to say is: there were no hair stylists, no salons, no combs or brushes, no barrettes, no myths about Rapunzel, no shampoos or any of the other myriad hair "products" you are no doubt familiar with, no Goldilocks, no adverse hirsute side effects of chemotherapy, no dyes, no Professor Corey jokes, no "bad hair" days, no unsaid questions and comparisons about hairweaves and straighteners and dyes, and furthermore no mustaches, beards or religious rules about men's facial peculiarities, no arguments about scarves. No Bluebeards. No Hercule Poirot. It was a world of shiny pates.

So, hairless, Lilith went along the road, singing to herself. (Lilith gets very bad press—you know how easily history can get re-written—but really, I can tell you two things about her most people don't know anymore: she wasn't any more of a demon than people usually are when everyone keeps tracking mud into the house, and she had a beautiful singing voice, which could, and did, tame the savage beast.)

She came to a river, which was blue, wide and very cold. She would need to ford it or swim it or hire a boat. No boatmen occurred. No obvious bridging methods appeared. The river, serenely running along, looked very blue, that particular blue that bespeaks ice in the bone when you enter it, so swimming seemed unattractive, though Lilith was always ready for adventure and took independent action on a daily basis, one thing that distinguished her from her later cousin (and sometime semblable) Eve. She continued to sing to herself as she contemplated her situation, since she found that often helped with cogitation, and besides, it was soothing.

As she sang, she walked along the edge of the river. Rushing and hurrying, and yet quite beautiful, it ran between its banks like a woman running a long way through a desert without thirst, and Lilith thought how beautiful the motion and curling of it, how the length and combing fingers of it soothed the earth, and that, even though it was preventing her from forward progress in her plan to visit her three children, it was like a woman. Though it had something, some running, fluid thing, that no woman had. (Or man, for that matter, though she did not, at this moment, I'm afraid, think about what men had. Having been born a woman, she tended to compare herself, when comparison came up, with things that made the world go round: water, wind, trees, bees making honey, etc.)

What is that? She thought. She was looking down at the river, and there, close to the bank, she saw river plants growing at the margin. Long strands, they waved and danced in the currents of the river, and seeing their long tendrils, she thought, *that is most beautiful.* And of a sudden moment (though of course all moments are sudden; it is simply that some seem to make much more of a splash than others) she thought, *now if I had a part of me that waved and rippled like that, it would add to my strength, it would augment my beauty, it would make me more like the world in all its wonder.* Now if this were a fairy story, Lilith would immediately find a way to make this magic. However, since this is only a how story—one of those stories that merely explains the way of the world—things do not travel on so famously or easily. The how of things always has an ache in it.

Whatever Lilith thought, the next thing that happened was that because she was so pre-occupied with the lovely curling and snaking of the plants, she lost her footing, and lickety-split, faster than you can pull any rabbit out of your hat—much faster, in fact—she fell into the water. Bald pate shining. Pretty arms flailing. Mouth, no longer full of music, instead full of water. She tumbled, she rolled, and around her she felt the cool tendrils and plaits of the water plants.

The plants thought her very beautiful and quite hysterical—for back in this time, it was news to no one that plants could think. Though annoyed by her splashing and heaving, they began, for the sake of her beauty, to figure out what she needed. "Air! She needs air!" shouted one plant whose fondness for CO_2 hadn't prevented her from studying the odd habits of mammals. But another one, whose intuitive capacities had always been admired by everyone, said, "but she wants to be one of us—she likes fluidity, she likes running, she wants tangle and curl! Grab her. Hold on!"

"Nonsense!" yelled another (plants in disagreement can really be quite argumentative) "—she'll drown if we don't get her on to land. Stop tangling her up!"

But with all the river water pouring downstream, and the plants waving and rippling, and Lilith gasping and rolling and swallowing water, the end came faster than one would have anticipated, and too soon and with a finality unsuited to the middle of a tale, there was Lilith, no longer breathing, rolling in the long, tangled fronds of the water plants at the wild river's edge. Drowned? you say. Oh no! How can this be?

But at this very moment, the eldest of her three children, Usir (later called Osiris and not famous for anything yet, and certainly not yet wise in the ways of the living and the dead, since he was only sixteen) turned up. At once, aghast, he pulled Lilith out of the water and tried to revive her. He pounded her chest and blew air into her mouth. He ordered her to wake up. She did not open her eyes. He began to weep. He pounded the ground. Around her head were wrapped the leaves and tangles of the river plants. "Oh river," he wailed. "Oh sun. Oh leaves and water, return me my mother, whose death is not yet ready. Change her, or mark her, but bring her back, oh please!" But nothing happened. Except that Lilith was turning blue, or more exactly greenish-purple. Usir ran off to find Orion, Lilith's second son, whom he'd left behind some bushes, setting a trap for rabbit. As yet Orion wasn't very good at catching game, and just now he was practicing a new method: snares, but as soon as Usir yanked him up, panting, yelling and pointing, he forgot all thought of rabbits, and lickety-split they both arrived back at Lilith's corpse, now a quite unlively shade of puce. Orion fell on his knees beside her, staring at the strange black stuff on her head. "Where the hell is Isis?" yelled Usir, who wanted his sister there, too. Orion stared down at his mother. "Oh jeez, oh jeez," (anachronistic as that may sound) he said. "Mom!" he yelled. Before this, she had always waked up when he yelled that loud.

"Isis!" wailed Usir, because he knew they all three, her children, needed to be there, if anything was to happen. And lo and behold his thirteen-year-old sister, Isis, who had been picking lotuses just down the way, came running up. And when she saw her mother all green and still, she grabbed her own cheeks and began to rock back and forth. "Quick, quick, stop that screeching, and come here," said Usir, who tended to order his younger sister about. This time she didn't argue. And then they all three wove their hands together and stood around Lilith, staring down at what looked much too much like a corpse, and each realized in that electrical moment that they would be scattered, limb from limb, heart from heart, that sky and water and indeed the dead, risen and wandering, would be their destinies.

Then Usir spoke again, the same words he had before, holding tight his brother and sister's hands, whom he had not yet lost to legend. "Oh river," he wailed. "Oh sun. Oh leaves and water, return me my mother, whose death is not yet ready. Change her, or mark her, but bring her back, oh please!" And because Usir's voice and love were so powerful, and because longing is in the motion of all things, and because the three of them were in it together—a rare conjunction—the river heard, and the plants of the river heard, and the flow and running of the river heard, and Lilith awoke. She gagged. She coughed. Water streamed from her mouth. She looked up and saw her children, constellations of all her sky.

And now, around her head, which had been formerly bald, was a wriggle and wrath of dark hair, running in ringlets and tangles, to signify that she was forever of the river, and that her life belonged now partly to water, partly to peril, and partly to wish.

She kissed Usir and Orion and Isis on their still-childish cheeks and touched her no longer bald pate. And suddenly on her children's heads too, fine hair sprouted, dark, red or blond, curly and straight, showing how all humans from now on would be partly river and daily reminded that tangle and flow, a confusion of outcomes, a tide and tangle of embellishment, were all part of the matter, which never, from one day to the next, could remain the same.

One of Those Days

It could have been a day when it rained lizards. Or frogs. Could have been, she supposed, if her eyes had still been tuned to that channel. Fire in the heavens making a hole in calendar expectations. A hole in the mirror through which your inevitable—and possibly fanged—twin stepped. At least a magic ring in the cereal. But no. Nowadays no lizards fell through the air; it just rained when it rained. Or she worried about the acid content of the precipitation.

One of the unpleasant effects of aging, she thought as she picked popcorn kernels off the couch: the constant laundry of life has taken away the shine and substituted, for the many and splendid, the daily news. Cleaning up. Something she'd done too many thousands upon thousands of times to find anything in it now but proof of entropy. Well, really. Nothing to complain about.

She wasn't particularly thinking of anything, or wanting anything. She certainly wasn't making a wish.

She plumped the wicker basket down in front of the dryer, began unloading the clothes. Scrabble, scrabble, toil and trouble, fire burn and cauldron... she picked up a pair of men's shorts, blue with a red lightning strike down one side and a large gold trident over the crotch, and stared at them. They were not her husband's—and furthermore, they had not been in the laundry she put into the washer. How had they...? Her eye lit on a lump of suspiciously leopard-skin fabric. It was a sock, male— at least she thought so—yellow, with black spots. Her husband would never wear anything remotely resembling either of these items. After a moment of stunned stillness, she pulled the rest of the clothes into the basket. One sock, the other... the usual towels, trousers, underpants, t-shirts, and there! a black t-shirt. On the back was the legend *Born to Ride*, with red jets of fire all around it. It dangled in air from her pinching fingers, big black and actual.

She stood over the basket, holding the thing well away, up at the level of her nose. Where had this stuff come from? She was used to laundry vagaries: missing socks, mysterious red streaks on things coming out of the dryer, every once in a while a guest's leftover something-or-other or a kid's swim trunks appearing when the family had all been over. But these things... it wasn't like that. They didn't belong to her, or to anyone she knew. Certainly not to Jaspar.

She smoothed the t-shirt and folded it carefully. She rolled the socks and laid them, with the shorts, on top of the shirt. She stood looking down on them, laid on top of the laundry pile.

"Excuse me," said a deep voice. She jumped. "Excuse me, please. Would you open this door?" The voice seemed to be coming from the laundry closet down the hall.

She did not faint or scream. She was not that kind. But she put her hand on the washer and thought seriously about sitting down in the laundry basket. While she was shaking her head, trying to clear it of this mirage, or whatever it was, there was a polite throat-clearing sound. "No need to worry. No harm intended, no worries. Just, I'd like to get my clothes, if you don't mind." The voice, firm, male and rather warm, sounded slightly inflected with an Indian lilt.

She thought of running downstairs and getting a broom, or a bat (but where was it, anyway, and did they actually still have one?) or maybe a knife but that would involve possible blood no no; she thought of grabbing the toilet plunger in the nearby bathroom for at least some brandishing, but she did none of these things. She stepped forward and opened the laundry closet. Obscuring the shelves of folded towels and sheets was a large man with curly black hair, a mustache of impressive proportions, and one of her own yellow towels wrapped around his waist.

"Good day," he said. "Or do you say good morning at this time of day hereabouts? I apologize for the abrupt arrival. Sometimes the transitions are, shall we say, poorly edited."

"Good god," she said. "Who are you? What are you doing in my laundry closet?"

He cleared his throat again. A slight flush appeared on his cheeks. "I am a genie."

"What?"

"I am a genie. I know it is a bit old-fashioned, that term. It's actually a corruption of jinni, a westernized version that came about... but I digress. As far as names go, I myself prefer genius to genie, but that departure from the traditional nomenclature is—"

"WHAT ARE YOU DOING IN MY CLOSET?"

He drew himself up to his full height, which was well over six feet, and frowned. His muscular shoulders seemed to bulge. "I will explain momentarily, madam. But really, I would appreciate it if you would give me my clothes. Please. And shut the door, so that I may make myself presentable."

She pushed the basket of clothes, with the strange ones on top, toward him with her foot, feeling oddly calm, but at the same time confused in a way she recognized from somewhere long ago, she couldn't think where. He picked up the clothes. She shut the laundry closet door. She considered running downstairs to the phone, but did not. Visions of loony bin allegations flitted by, unregarded, (after all, she'd managed, despite all odds, to grow up noticeably sane) while she just stood there, staring at the laundry closet door. After a bit of shuffling, he knocked, and she opened the door again. There he was, a large brownish man in leopard-skin socks, loud shorts and black t-shirt. His legs, she noticed inconsequentially, were free of hair. Unlike Jaspar's.

"Where are my pants? Please."

She found the black sweats she hadn't noticed before and handed them over. He pulled them on.

"Now then." He stepped forward and held out his hand. "My name is Jam."

She stared.

"Well, Jamil, really. How do you do."

She couldn't help it. She shook his hand. He bowed, and waited.

"Uh. Well. Mine is Heather." This seemed a concession of some sort. She hoped the heat in her cheeks didn't mean she was blushing.

"Pleased to make your acquaintance, Madam, though of course I already know your name. Now then. Where are your requests?"

"My requests?"

He frowned again. "Perhaps we are having cultural difficulties here. I do prefer written requests. In triplicate. I am a very fast reader, lightning-fast in fact, so you will not need to wait very long, although—" he glanced around at the hall, the alcove with the washing machine, the clothes piled on the floor, "I don't really see any suitable place for burning them."

"Burning…?"

"The requests." He sighed, in what appeared to be a longsuffering way. "Apparently you're not listening. Is there a fireplace?"

She found herself speechless. She narrowed her eyes, trying to assume a look of suspicion, or at least skepticism. It was somehow hard to muster the appropriate level of distress.

A sound of thunder drew her eyes momentarily to the window at the end of the hall. The visible sky was an ominous purple; a crackle of lightning jolted her. She was sure this weather was a sudden apparition.

He glanced down the hall as thunder rolled. "Don't go out tonight. There's a bad moon on the right."

She couldn't help it. "Don't you mean 'on the rise?'"

"Pardon me?"

"It's not 'there's a bad moon on the right,' it's 'there's a bad moon on the rise.'"

"No matter. This moon is in any case on the right. And you shouldn't go out tonight. It's bound to take your something or other. Nasty weather."

"What?" Now she was scared. "Who are you? What do you mean?"

"I told you. My name's Jamil. I am not here to scare you. For pity's sake, Madam, kindly adhere to the protocol. I am merely trying to help." Nonetheless, what looked like thunderclouds almost as black as the ones outdoors began to gather over his eyes. "Really," he continued in a rising tone while she stood frozen, "must we stand here in the hall jawing away like gangbusters when I am merely responding to your summons, present—as usual!—in trying circumstances, attempting merely to do my job while a storm of massive proportions is coming on and I haven't *even had my breakfast?*"

She cleared her throat. Perhaps best to humor him and get downstairs, where the doors and the phone were. "Jamal, I—"

"Please, Madam! Either you are not listening, or I am afraid you have the usual American tin ear!" He rolled his eyes. "It's not Jam*al*! Jamal means 'camel,' and may I point out that I am not a beast of burden! My name is Jami-i-i-l!"

He stared down at her. She backed away slowly. He sighed. "I see I've frightened you. Please accept my apologies. But this kind of misunderstanding, may I say, is exactly why I suggested you call me Jam. Now then." He stepped forward and rubbed his hands together. "Do you have any scrambled eggs?"

She swallowed and nodded. Okay. Downstairs. She turned, the back of her neck prickling, and walked down the stairs. She heard nothing on the stairs behind her and, halfway down, turned to look. He was right behind her, skimming along lightly as a ballerina. In fact, if she hadn't felt it was a crazy thought—though why anything should seem crazy at this moment she couldn't say—she could have sworn he was floating down the stairs. He smiled encouragingly. She whipped down the rest of the stairs and into the kitchen, but before she could get to the back door, there he was, standing with his arms crossed over his considerable chest, between the door and the kitchen table, smiling. Behind him the sky, in the kitchen door window, roiled.

She didn't know what else to do. She opened the refrigerator and, watching her own untrembling hand, which really didn't give her any useful ideas, took out the carton of eggs.

"Um, okay. Scrambled, you said?"

"Perfect. Do you have any sumac or garlic?"

The bowl clanged as she got it out of the cabinet, and she jumped. "Sumac? Isn't that a poisonous plant?" She did not glance over her shoulder.

"No, no, madam, it's a spice. Very tasty. Well, just garlic then. You do have garlic?"

Now she turned around, the iron frying pan in one hand, the metal bowl in the other. Sunnily, he said, "everyone, even here, has garlic." Whacking him with the frying pan didn't seem especially wise, so she turned back, put the pan on the stove and began whipping up the eggs.

He ate half a dozen scrambled eggs and four pieces of whole wheat toast, sitting opposite her at the kitchen table, his back to the door. How he ate wasn't entirely clear. She set the plate down in front of him and turned to get a fork out of the drawer. When she turned back, the plate was clean. She was beginning to wonder if she was having some trouble with her vision. Or her time sense. He beamed. He wiped his mouth on the napkin she laid down next to the shining plate. He towered. His mustache and hair were an unearthly and dense black, the kind of black she associated with old Italian or Filipino or Cuban or... whatever, people whose hair color had been very dark in youth... and then when they were old but unready for the gray, came inky out of a bottle. He smiled; his teeth were shiny. She was beginning to feel dizzy, so she sat down opposite him. It appeared the world around her had gone nuts, even if she hadn't.

"Delicious. Thank you. I am sure that will improve my mood. I do apologize, madam, for the prandial interruption. As you no doubt know, we—er—genies exact no actual payment, so I hope you will be kind enough to consider this a donation. For the good of us both, of course." He rose to his full height just as a particularly loud clap of thunder actually shook the house. "Now. Let us get down to business." He glanced out the window. "Hmm. I fear rivers may be overflowing. But no matter. Your requests, Madam."

But she had had enough.

She got up. "Please leave now. I don't know who you are or how you got in my house, but it's time to go now. I have given you breakfast, and I have been polite,

I, I haven't called the police because you seem, well, you seem... a bit..." She stopped. "Please go."

A very strong odor filled the air. Bitter cherries, musk, some smoky flavor she couldn't place. Her knees felt weak. He didn't move. The inner corners of his black eyebrows went up slightly, as a child's will do when he or she is upset and about to cry.

He sighed, a long windy exhalation. She sat down suddenly, feeling she'd been blown into her chair by some reluctance originating inside her. "Madam,"—and was his voice actually a bit shaky? —"I can see we have somehow gotten off on a bad foot here." He put one palm down on the table next to his plate and there, next to his hand, was a sheaf of papers she was sure hadn't been there before. "Let me reiterate." He picked up the papers and waved them over the plate, vaguely in her direction. "I am only here because you called. I cannot leave—those are the rules under which we jinn live, you see, and I assure you it is a well-structured universe, the invisible one flowing between and around every moment you live in your oh so tasty one"—he rolled his eyes—"by tasty I only mean to compliment you on your culinary skills, I assure you, no other implications intended—let's see, where was I? oh yes, the rules. I cannot leave, you see, once you have called, until I hear or read your request—we no longer refer to them as 'wishes', very old-fashioned idea, the wish idea, since not all of them... but I digress again. I'm afraid that you have rather thrown me off. These constant misunderstandings are so... I am feeling just a bit...—" he sniffed. "Let me collect myself, Madam." And he turned his back. It looked as though he was wiping his nose or his eyes on his t-shirt. In spite of herself, she felt a bit curious about the sheaf of papers. Could it actually be something she'd written?

"Oh, for god's sake," she said. "Don't cry."

"I never cry," he said loudly, and, raising his face like a dog sniffing air, marched off into the living room. "The fireplace. We can examine your requests there."

She got up and followed him into the living room. His presence tinged everything—the furniture, the walls, the carpet she never even saw any more—with the bright colors of shock, or revelation—or was it disorder? Water streamed down the windows, rain drummed on the roof. All around, the universe—at least the local one that belonged to her—was enclosed in a storm of electrifying proportions. A flash of lightning. Thunder growled and cracked. Something slapped against the front window. Bits of leaf and twig squirmed against the glass. What had the weather prediction been for today? A rain of lizards after all?

Jamil—yes, she might as well accept it, he did have a name—was standing in front of the fireplace, peering at the papers, which he held at arm's length. "I have somehow misplaced my glasses, I'm afraid, but I can see you haven't written anything down yet, Mrs. Heather. Well, no matter. No need, actually, to put it in triplicate.

I mean, we jinn do prefer detailed reports—the more we see of the various circumstances, the archipelago of wish as it were, the better the precisions of fulfillment. But then, not everyone wants to write for hours and hours only to have it read in a second. And—" he dropped his hand and gazed at her, his brow wrinkled—"you are obviously unfamiliar with the protocol, being trapped in this faraway and historically-ahem—perhaps ignorant is too strong a word—land. Strike that, strike that. Polite is definitely my policy, though not all jinn would appreciate the difficulties of... well, well. I'll let the written part go, as a gesture of hands-across-the-sea. Protocol to the winds!" And he flicked the papers into air. They floated to the floor. "Be relaxed, I beg you, Madam. You can just tell me, in your own words, what it is you wish. Request, I mean."

For a moment she just stood there. But this particular universe, enclosed by thunderclaps and squirming twigs (*were* those lizards?) on the windows, despite its many peculiarities and its destabilizing echoes of cataclysm, had begun to seem interesting. Well, down the rabbit hole, after all. She subsided on to the couch.

"Hmm. Requests. Let's see." She tapped her fingers together. Why not? "Would you mind sitting down, please? I can't think with you looming like that."

"Your wish is my command." He grinned. "Little joke." He sat down in the big green arm-chair Jaspar liked. He looked about twice as large as Jaspar, but somehow, at this moment, his face reminded her of a bunny's. Or was it a cat?

"Let's see. I'd have to think about what—" She narrowed her eyes. Suddenly all the stories rushed back into her consciousness. "How does this work? What do *you* get in return?"

He looked hurt. Thunder rolled and the wind tried to stuff itself down the chimney. "Madam. Please. I get nothing. This is my job. I go where I'm called. I do what is expected. I—"

"In the stories I can remember at the moment, in or out of a bottle, genies are a dangerous species, and wishes always come with strings attached."

"Ah." Now he smiled. "You are looking for a philosophical, philological and cosmic discussion. Nothing I like more. Well, except for... But really, that would take quite a bit of time, Madam. Which we may not have." Now he frowned. "But if you have a few specific questions, I would be glad to answer them. Though an atmosphere of doubt is not my favorite..."

"There's the Fisherman's Wife. That didn't go well."

"Well, greed, for pity's sake, Madam! That's the moral of that story! And that, after all, was a flounder, not a genie! In any case, we all know that greed is a constant difficulty—in any world under the sun. As it were. Some worlds are not really under the sun, I hasten to..." He cleared his throat. "One difference between jinn and humans, Madam, is that humans' eyes are much bigger than their biceps."

"I think you mean stomachs."

"Stomachs?"

"Not biceps."

"No, I mean biceps. Jinn are very strong." He pumped one arm; his bicep bulged. "Much stronger than your strongest strong man."

She squinted. "But I don't really see what that has to do with..." Oh oh, she thought, I'm actually not making any sense any more, either... "What I'm asking about," she said firmly, "is what you expect of me in return. What's the fly in the ointment?"

He looked around. "Ointment? I have provided no ointments. Was it some sort of unguent you wanted?"

She sighed. "We seem to be at cross purposes here. I just want to know if there's some catch. If I ask you for something—"

"If you finally get down to business, Madam, and ask me for something—and may I remind you that my time is valuable, I am on assignment here and just trying to make a little progress in the matter at hand—I can assure you *there will be no fly in any ointment I provide!*" He took a deep breath. "So sorry. Volume control is a weakness. Size differentials."

Silence.

"Look. We jinn have many communities, a variety of temperaments according to our place in the cosmic panoply, and a number of different national narratives... So your reading may have given you, let us say, an indistinct—or narrow might be a better word—impression of the consequences of contact between our two... worlds. If you are foolish enough to call on a jinni and then refuse his help, well. I really can't be responsible for the loss you will suffer. It is a tremendous accomplishment, you know, to bridge these two worlds. Yours, I must admit, as well as mine. Now." He put his palms together, closed his eyes and breathed in and out a few times in what looked like a self-calming ritual. "Shall we get down to effing business?"

More silence. "Excuse my German."

She sighed. "You mean French."

"Whatever."

"Where are you actually from? Los Angeles?"

"No more questions. Please tell me what is wrong that I may fix."

"Okay. Well." Her feeling of collaboration had faded. The weird intimacy of the conversation had begun, in fact, to make her suspect herself of a screw-loose stupidity. Perhaps if she humored him, she could get him to leave. She glanced toward the front window, where numerous jetsam had plastered itself against the glass. The rain had stopped, though the sky was still an eggplant color she'd never seen mid-afternoon before.

"Well. The main thing, really, is meaning." Now why had she said that?

"Meaning? Do you mean the cosmic spiral or the hierarchical ladder?" He beamed.

"No, no. I mean my own life. Existential, I suppose."

"Ah. What is it, then, if I may ask, that would give it meaning?"

She thought. "Well, it used to be the inherent magic of things, the possibility of—"

She stared at him. He grinned. It was a thunderclap grin. Or was that the storm beginning again? Rain poured down in buckets. Applying the word 'sudden' would not suffice.

"Well, we don't need to worry about that one anymore, do we?"

"I'm not sure I meant—"

"Be that as it may. In any case, we are talking not about the past, but about the future. And please, let us be a bit more specific. We are not here for a philosophical discussion. What is your request?" And he leaned forward and spread his arms out as though the whole world that was hers lay before them, ready for a glory of change.

She actually thought about it. He was a bit irresistible, and anyway she couldn't seem to make him go away. Maybe this would do it.

"Well, my personal life—" she hesitated, not wanting to implicate Jaspar, who was after all a decent man, and most definitely not wanting to suggest that he couldn't handle an intruder if he happened to come home about now— "is a bit... humdrum."

"Ah, humdrum. In all worlds, the new becomes the accustomed. The exciting becomes... something else."

She nodded, feeling an upwelling of unfamiliar longing, along with some stinging behind her eyes.

"Hmmm. And what is it that needs alteration? Or replacement?" He leaned forward.

Oh dear. A dangerous tack. Had she made an errant wish or two, after all?

"Nothing! Nothing needs replacement. Perhaps the carpet in the guest bedroom..."

"Madam! I am not a carpet salesman! Please do me the honor of telling me the truth! We are having an important conversation here, and your requests are just beginning to come into focus!" Thunder rolled. Rain slashed at the window. This conversation had gotten out of hand. Though one not so small part of her wanted to go on with the definition of her longing, the other part, the foursquare part—the one Jaspar called down-to-earth, a completely attractive quality, in his view—took control.

"My husband may come home any minute. After all, this weather—"

"Don't worry." He smiled; his face crinkled warmly. "We are quite safe, Madam, here in the comfort of our very interesting colloquy. No need to worry about sudden interruptions. I have put a seal – no matter. We do not need to discuss jinn engineering, which I assure you outstrips most human efforts, here and now at any rate." He leaned forward. "I intend no undue familiarity, but perhaps, given the nature of our conversation, I should call you Heather? Or would Mrs. Heather be more respectful?"

The weather, both inside and out, was so unfamiliar as to leave her little foursquareness to spare. She sighed. "Heather will be okay."

He beamed. "Well. Good. Then, Heather, back to the business at hand. Things are already in motion here. The spring, from which the river flows, bubbles up. What exactly needs alteration in your present humdrum existence? Specifics, clearly stated, are required—I mean of course, very helpful—in these matters."

She looked away, toward the window plastered with foreign bodies. A longing to say it out loud—to name it at last—arose inside her. To tell him. This conversation, whatever world in which it was taking place, would never go anywhere besides in one ear and out the other of her odd visitor.

"Jaspar—that's my husband—doesn't understand me."

"So you are wishing for understanding? For someone to understand you?"

"Not someone. Jaspar."

"He does not know how to understand? He is lacking in capacity?" Jamil frowned, whether at her or at Jaspar's failings she could not tell.

"It's not a matter of capacity. I don't think. Perhaps he's not—"

"Very smart?"

"No, no! He's quite smart! That's not—"

"Strong enough to pass the barrier into your world?"

"That is not what I mean. It's not a matter of smart or strong. That's all fine." A brief and unwanted picture of Jaspar's slack stomach and slightly stooping, now, shoulders, flashed into her mind. "I mean he's not interested. Any more. Or something."

"Ah." His face cleared of weather, became calm, pacific. "You mean the sapience."

"Sapience?"

"The scorching fires of knowledge."

"Scorching fires? Nothing scorching here. I am talking about interest. In another person's..." she sighed "...inner life. Or something."

"You keep saying 'or something.' That is not a very specific phrase. How am I to quantify this 'or something?'" He leaned forward. "In fact, let us be clear. The fires of knowledge can be, though I know it is not a thought that is everywhere welcome, scorching. Are we not talking about passion, and the humdrum, its utter nemesis?" He was tapping his fingers on the arm of the chair. In some kind of similar rhythm, the rain lashed the windows. Thunder walked the roof.

"Well, maybe. I think what I meant was..." Her voice trailed away.

"Whatever you would call it, it must be the opposite of humdrum! That is your own word! Humdrum! You need the wisdom of breaking through! The new! The alive! Is that not it?" He leaned forward, his eyes glittering. "I can help you with this. Only tell me in your own words. I must have a request. Tell me."

His eyes seemed both fierce and soft. This confused her.

"Well, really, it's probably not a problem with Jaspar. He is, after all..." She shook herself. "Okay. So it's not Jaspar's fault the world grows..."

"So right, dear lady! Jaspar is not the point here! It is of you, Madam—I mean Heather—I am speaking! It is you, and your life we are discussing! You and me, in the midst of the world's total glory!" He glanced at the window. "Madam! Your wish is forming here between us. Things are in motion already! Only say!" A lightning flash made the room blue. On the window every bit of strange life sticking to the surface stood out in black. Inside her, a bolus, a clatch, a brimming basket of wishes boiled up and overflowed. An earthquake, in which all the paths she hadn't taken and the experiences she hadn't had, and the moments in which the world had put on dull clothes and hid itself in a disguise she only now came to recognize was not its true form, split open and into sight, and there it was: her wish.

She looked into Jamil's very black eyes.

"I want to be—" she just missed saying "in love again," realizing that would imply some problem with Jaspar "—swept away again" she finished.

His eyes shone dark and bright. Reminding her of agate, or even—lightning! a jolt she felt in her bones. She felt mesmerized. She became aware of her own hands rubbing the rough cloth of the couch next to her thighs. "—is that—" and then, knowing she had almost finished the sentence "—too much to ask?—" she snapped out of it. What a dreadfully, stupidly childish and narcissistic wish. Love was not a series of thunderclap swoons. What could she be thinking? Worse, what could she be revealing about herself to this perfect stranger, some hopefully harmless lunatic who—thunder cracked its whip. The house actually shook, and beneath her the couch trembled as though it were alive.

"There it is at last!" Jamil raised one arm triumphantly. "A wish! And a well-formed one, meant to lead us right into—that is, I mean of course a request. Not a wish." He beamed. "Well done, Madam Heather!" (she had time, in all her confusion, to think *Madame Heather?* and reject a correcting remark) "Well done!"

"Wait! I didn't mean—wait! Love is not a series of thunderclap swoons..."

"My dear lady! Of course it is!" He rubbed his hands together. "Let us get down to business."

"Wait! I—I didn't mean..."

"Madam Heather!" He frowned and grinned at once. "Once a wish, always a wish! But no time for retrograde motions, and anyway Mercury is flying ever closer to the sun at this very moment, while Venus hovers above us, so there is no time to lose."

He rose. He picked up all the papers spread on the carpet and put them in the fireplace. He took the matches from the box on the mantel and lit them. A thin smoke went up the chimney, and POOF was blown back down into the room by a gust of wind. She breathed in a bloom of smoky fragrance, something like new-mown grass, something like mushrooms, in the back of her throat a sting of sharpness. She coughed. Her eyes watered, and for a moment the room slid and blurred.

Jamil bowed. "I wish you a warm goodbye, Madam. It is time now for me to depart. The first—and might I add, most important—part of our work is done." And much to her surprise, he strode out of the room without a backward glance. She heard the front door open and close. And just like that, he was gone.

She sat on the couch, staring into the stillness. It seemed to her in that moment that the future had collapsed into a sudden diminished version of the present, which had become an odd dream punctuated by thunder and purple skies. Everything in the room looked drab, colorless, though against the window silvered by wet, black bodies squirmed like a prediction of doom. Thunder purred and grumbled.

After a good while in which very little occurred to her and rain drummed steadily on the roof and in her skull, she rose. She went into the kitchen. There was the licked-clean plate. She washed it. She checked the eggs. Yes. Half a dozen gone. She went upstairs. There was the laundry basket. No interloping clothes. She folded the familiar laundry and put it away.

As the afternoon wore on, she thought about going out, but did not. She thought about checking online for the weather report, but did not. Lightning flashed and she heard a rush and gurgle of waters as though rivers were running in the street. She didn't look. "Don't go out tonight, it's bound to take your..."—it wasn't "something or other." It was *life*. The wind slammed and banged; she wondered if the roof would fly off. She thought about calling Jaspar. It was a bad day for driving, and soon he'd be on the freeway. She thought of calling her daughter. Or her best friend. She did none of these things. All intention had left her, as though her so-called wish had drained her of energy for the future.

At 4:30 PM the phone rang. Jaspar's voice was thin, reedy, behind a rushing sound like a waterfall. "Heather?"

"Jaspar! Thank God! This weather—"

"Look, Heather. I'm sorry. I'm sorry to tell you like this." A crackle of static. "I'm not coming home."

"What?" She cupped her hand around the phone. "Is the highway—"

"I'm not coming home."

"What? What are you talking about? Jaspar, are you all ri—"

"I've decided to go away."

"Go away? Where are you—"

"It makes no difference where I am, Heather. I could be in another world. In fact, I am in another world. I'm going away with Lorraine. From the office."

"Lorraine? Did you say Lorraine? What?" For a moment she couldn't grasp it. Jaspar didn't even like Lorraine, as far as she knew, and Lorraine certainly wasn't his type. "What are you—" Inconsequentially, she thought of *rivers overflowing*, of *bound to*—at least he was alive. She squeezed her eyes shut against the thoughts.

"I should have told you before. But you must have known for a long time that something was wrong. And now we're—"

"Jaspar! Don't go out tonight!" There was a crackle of thunder, and in her hand the phone grew hot, turned blue. She dropped it. She stared at her hand, which was not burned. From the phone on the floor came a small voice, growing dimmer. She couldn't quite make out the words—something about going, about sorry, maybe the word "coward," then a click, quite loud, and the faint insect buzz of a dial tone. She touched the phone, which was no longer blue, with her foot. She stared at it. Out of that phone had come smoke, then fire, then the sound of far space, and that was that.

She shook herself. For a moment she thought about how she could find him, stop him, get him to hole up somewhere, away from... what? She poured herself a glass of wine and sat down on the couch to clear her mind of the after-effects. Surely the motions of the universe did not comply with her inner motions. She wished... no, no, she wished nothing! And Jaspar! This desertion in the midst of chaos was not, somehow, believable. Lorraine? This, all of this, just couldn't be! Her cheeks grew wet. Sadly, she went over the ways of division and discontinuity and loss her own life offered for contemplation. Her own selfhood a cautionary tale.

An hour later, she heard someone at the front door and ran into the hallway. He'd changed his mind! Her eyes grew large with the shock, the unexpected expected standing again at her door, the wish rushing in out of the blue. There he was. Behind his shoulders stormless sky gleamed. He swept her up, his dark eyes glittering, and lifted her off her feet. She felt his strange black black hair on her cheek, his mustache a thicket of heat on her neck. "I'm home, darling Mrs.! I'm home at last! Let's not go out tonight!"

Acknowledgments

"The Seventh Blue" was a finalist for the 2009 Reynolds
    Price Short Story Award and appeared online in
    AbleMuse

"Memory of the Future" appeared in *Fabulist Words & Art*

"Fable with Wings" appeared in *Unlikely Stories*

And thanks to...

...the un-named others and ancestors over the centuries who told stories, whether written or not, about the ways humans and other animals and the elements interact and come to know each other. To Jorge Luis Borges, Italo Calvino and Virginia Woolf, who showed me the way to dwell in the liminal and how to jump sideways. And to the ancient sagas, which moved within, and every poet, so many I can't name them, who helped me visit that central place where connection resides, and who understood how language is music is incantation. To all the writers who have helped to sustain and teach me, both the ones I have read and the ones I've known, beginning with Jackson Burgess at the University of California Berkeley and going on to the poet Don Schenker, and including Iris Barbura and Alan Grow, who taught me the same thing in movement and energy, not words. Thanks so much to the writers I know who have been so important in my life and in sustaining the pleasures of the mind & heart: including Alev Croutier, a deep and valuable friendship, and Grace Grafton and Ramsay Bell Breslin, who have been such close and helpful companions, and the other members of my poetry group: Carol Dorf, Kathleen McClung, Tobey Kaplan, and Catherine Freeling, with whom creative exchange has been so exciting, (poetry and prose are not always so different), a warm thanks to the inspiring Harriet Chessman and Maw Shein Win, and a special thanks to Thaisa Frank, whose astounding work and valued friendship has often made me happy to be, after all, a writer. I must include the visual artists I know, with whom my dialogue has always been so fertile, especially Bruce Katz, Liz Ennis, Alice Schenker, whom I miss, and Jeff Long. And a heartfelt thanks to the inimitable Jonathan Penton of Unlikely Books, who has been just plain wonderful to work with on this book. Last but not least, my family: to my Aunt Giggi (Charlotte Hiller), who told me colorful stories and dreams as a child, and finally, to my beloved present family, without whom my life would not have its bedrock and flourish, and of course to Phillip, whose recognition helped make me myself—and for all those great dinners, too.

About the Author

Tobey Hiller was born on the east coast and migrated west many years ago. She lives in Northern California, where she worked for many years as a psychodramatist, group leader/consultant, teacher, and therapist. She and her  husband have two children and four grandchildren, and she counts her large, lively and talkative extended family as a main inspiration and life teaching. She has always been interested in myths, legends and fables, and in the edge zones where melt, collision or transformation occur. Hence this collection of odd tales. She can't resist the skeleton that story gives to every move we make.

In addition to her poetry and nonfiction work, she writes both realist and fabulist fiction. Her story "Splinter" won First Prize in *Craft*'s 2020 Short Story Elements Contest and was earlier short-listed for the first Los Gatos-Listowel Short Story Contest; "The Seventh Blue" was a finalist for the Reynolds Price Short Fiction Award; two of her other stories have been short-listed for prizes, and this fiction collection *Flight Advice: a fabulary* was one of five finalists for *Omnidawn*'s Fabulist Fiction Prize (2019) under the name *Particle to Wave: a fabulary*. Photo by Robert Croutier.

Other Books by Tobey Hiller

Poetry

Crossings (Oyez, 1980)

Certain Weathers (Oyez, 1987)

Aqueduct (Clear Mountain Press, 1993, with drawings by
    Joanna Axtmann)

Crow Mind (Finishing Line Press, 2020)

Novel

Charlie's Exit (Edgework, 2003)

Nonfiction

*Recreating Partnership: A Solution-Oriented, Collaborative
    Approach to Couples Therapy* (W.W. Norton, 2001,
    with her husband Phillip Ziegler)

Recent Titles from Unlikely Books

A Brief Conversation with Consciousness by Marc Vincenz

~getting away with everything by Vincent A. Cellucci and Christopher Shipman

fata morgana by Joel Chace

Typescenes by Rodney A. Brown

Political AF: A Rage Collection by Tara Campbell

The Deepest Part of Dark by Anne Elezabeth Pluto

Swimming Home by Kayla Rodney

Manything by dan raphael

Citizen Relent by Jeff Weddle

The Mercy of Traffic by Wendy Taylor Carlisle

Cantos Poesia by David E. Matthews

Left Hand Dharma: New and Selected Poems by Belinda Subraman

Apocalyptics by C. Derick Varn

Pachuco Skull with Sombrero: Los Angeles, 1970 by Lawrence Welsh

Monolith by Anne McMillen (Second Edition)

When Red Blood Cells Leak by Anne McMillen (Second Edition)

My Hands Were Clean by Tom Bradley (Second Edition)

anonymous gun. by Kurtice Kucheman (Second Edition)

Soy solo palabras but wish to be a city by Leon De la Rósa, illustrated by Gui.ra.ga7 (Second Edition)

Blue Rooms, Black Holes, White Light by Belinda Subraman

www.ingramcontent.com/pod-product-compliance
Lightning Source LLC
Chambersburg PA
CBHW030132260626
47156CB00008B/2915